ALORA 2.0

ROMANCE REBOOTED

Gloria C. Bishop

Dedication

In my life I have had the pleasure of having wonderful male role models who have taught me how a man should treat a woman. They inspired me to create strong male characters that have their flaws but are real and lovable.

Dad. Although we share no blood, you have loved me as much as your biological children and for that alone I will always hold you as my Dad. You have been there for me since I was a young child and I wouldn't trade you for the world. You taught me that love, that family isn't about blood. That men can have a sense of humour and that standing by a woman through all the changes in life is normal. Love you, always.

Lloyd. We have had a rocky relationship over the years and didn't always understand one another. However these last few years we've become much closer and I cherish the relationship that we have developed. You have taught me that redemption is never out of reach. That fathers and daughters can reconnect as adults and develop healthy relationships. Thank you.

Gord. My one and only father-in-law. Your presence and sense of humour is one of the things that I loved about you from the moment we met. You taught me that a man could be military strong and still show emotions. I miss you.

$\mathcal{A}$cknowledgements

As always I have so many people to thank. First always is my family. Bill and the kids show me every day how they accept me and are willing to allow me to be the crazy artistic person I am. You are never far from my mind or my heart.

To the Imagined Writers Group, you give me support and inspiration that I often need. Thank you.

To Tracy and Shannon, thank you for letting me be part of you. You are both truly my sisters from other misters. Together we can do anything. I can't wait to retire and move into our senior's home. Love you both so very much.

To all the geeks out there, who attend Fan Expo or just hide their appreciation of all things geek. Thank you. You are my peeps and I wrote this one for you. Thank you.

Finally to all my readers. Without you these books that I have written would just sit on a shelf collecting dust. I write for me, because I have to write or die but I also write for you. Your enjoyment, encouragement and laughter is always appreciated and keeps me motivated.

Chapter 1

"Dammit, Cass! I can't breathe!" Alora huffed as she tried to inhale. "This corset was a bad idea! The whole thing is a bad idea!"

"Quit your bitchin', it'll be fine. I just have to get it done up, and then you'll feel better." Cass muttered from behind Alora, as she tied the laces. "There, done." She tapped Alora's shoulder. "Now turn around, I've gotta check the fit."

The laces had loosened off slightly and Alora could take shallow breaths without injury. She turned around and faced her little sister.

While Cass fussed with the waist line Alora glanced at her. The past few years had been good to Cass, she'd managed to shed the anxiety ridden anorexia that had tortured her all through high school and now looked womanly and soft. Shorter than Alora, with a beautiful shade of auburn hair cut in a short asymmetrical pixie style which showcased high cheekbones and Disney like wide brown eyes. College had increased Cass's self-confidence and allowed her creativity to flow, as clearly evidenced by what Alora wore. The pride she felt in her sister overwhelmed her at times, and occasionally she couldn't believe that she was the same girl who had plagued her all through their childhood.

Cass' eyes narrowed professionally as she looked up and down the skin tight black costume. "Put the mask on." She demanded.

Alora fumbled with the face piece until Cass sighed and slapped her hands away. "Let me, you klutz."

After a few more minutes of tugging and adjusting, Cass stood back, and again stared at her. The silence stretched for so long that Alora felt butterflies begin to flutter in her tightly bound stomach.

"Do I look that bad?" Alora questioned quietly.

"What?" Cass' eyes flew up to meet Alora's. "No, of course not. You look hot, big sis. A total knock out. I was just assessing my stitch work."

"So, can I look now?" Alora tried to arch an eyebrow, but the full head mask prevented her from moving her face the way she normally would.

Cass nodded and moved away from the full-length mirror attached to the wall behind her. Alora closed her eyes and with a, necessarily shallow, but steadying breath she looked at the reflection.

Her eyes widened with shock, she couldn't even tell who looked back at her. Slowly she started an observation that began with her feet, which were encased in super glossy black leather boots, the heels made her four inches taller than her normal five foot four inches. Her body looked svelte in the shiny pleather pants and corset top, with thick white stitching placed in a seemingly random pattern. While the top was a turtleneck style, the placement of the stitches somehow made her breasts look much bigger than normal, that and the corset lacing the back pulled her body in, in ways she couldn't have imagined possible.

Her hair was hidden entirely by the head mask, its gleaming surface reflecting the light in the room. Bright, blood red lipstick coated her lips and made a splash of colour in the otherwise dark ensemble. Her blue eyes even looked a different shape than normal thanks to the black makeup she wore.

She twisted to look at the back, impressed with how the lacings that started at her tailbone on the pants, lined up perfectly with the corset, making the whole outfit appear to be a single bodysuit. She smiled with appreciation at Cass' skill, before she turned and again looked at her face. Tilting her head, she decided the costume somehow managed to hide all her flaws but emphasize her qualities; she definitely didn't look average in this.

She grinned, thrilled at the transformation. Overall she didn't look like herself, she looked like Catwoman. Michelle Pfeiffer's' Catwoman to be exact.

"Wow." She whispered. "Cass this is gorgeous! You did such a great job."

"Thanks. You look seriously hot." Cass smiled, her light brown eyes crinkling with joy.

"Now I just have to get up the nerve to go out in public in this." Alora laughed.

"Hey! There's no backing out. You begged me to make it, and I spent over forty hours on that damn costume. Do you have any idea how difficult it is to work with PVC? You are going to that convention if I have to shove you through the door."

"I know. I know." She stressed, "I'm just nervous." This was Aloras second time attending a comic convention. Last years' Fan Expo had been a real eye opener; she loved the costumes, the people, the everything. She found that fans of all sorts of different genres came, not just comic book fans as she had originally thought.

She had had such a great time, the most fun she'd had in years, and she had vowed to come back, dressed up this year. Although her geekdom typically didn't include Catwoman or comics for that matter, she had given Cass free artistic license to make whatever she wanted as long as Alora fit in, without looking like a complete dork and even she had to admit what Cass had come up with far exceeded all expectations.

"I still wish you were coming with me." She muttered allowing her nerves free reign for a moment.

Cass nodded. "Me too. I've never been to a con, and after what you described I wish I could go with you. But, being that we're in the big city for only two days I must get to the fashion district. The fabrics are to die for!" She sighed with genuine happiness. "Honestly, Alora I can't wait to dig my fingers into some of the Egyptian linens I've heard about."

"You are such a fabric whore!" Alora laughed as Cass nodded her head in total agreement.

"A silk slut, I just can't help myself. I also have plans tonight to get together with some college friends. Are you sure you're going to be fine by yourself, or do you wanna tag along?"

"No." Alora shook her head, the mask making the movement feel unusual. "I'll be fine. There's an after party that I want to hit up." Besides that, Alora knew she definitely didn't want to be the third wheel with her kid sisters plans. She intended to let loose where no one knew her, her family, or her sordid tale of misspent youth. And most important no one knew her latest humiliations. She shoved thoughts of Wendell from her mind, focusing instead on other reasons to tear it up in Toronto.

As much as she loved her family, being from a smaller town where she constantly got recognized as 'one of the Mcintoshs' became very tiresome. Coming from a family of five kids, each who had their own set of activities and foibles, made it hard to hide who she was for any length of time. It seemed like everyone had 'heard of' or 'met' or 'knew' at least one of the Mcintoshs.

In Kennedy, Ontario there was no place to hide. Like the whole 'Cheers' theme song, 'where everybody knew your name,' except for Alora it felt like everyone knew not only her name but everything about her and her family. It had gotten better in the past few years as the town expanded and she had hidden in her studio, however whenever she left the house she still felt the stares.

"Coolio, but if your plans fall through, just text me and you can meet up with us." Cass moved up beside Alora. "As requested, I put a small pocket in each glove, one for your hotel key, ID and such. The other side will hold some cash. And there's this pocket inside your boot to put your cell phone." She demonstrated each hidden pocket as she talked.

It had been one of Aloras demands that the pockets be there, she didn't want to carry a purse or bag since it would totally ruin the look of the costume. After filling the pockets Alora took a final look in the mirror, grabbed her bullwhip, and with a confidence she didn't feel, she waved goodbye to Cass. Grabbing her courage by the proverbial balls she exited the hotel to catch the subway.

***

Dillon stepped to one side with a pleasant nod, allowing the Storm Troopers to pass through the loud, packed aisle. Fans swarmed the area, creating a cacophony of noise. The babble of thousands of voices, music and laughter surrounded him, cradling him in warmth and a comfortable sense of camaraderie.

He had wandered into the largest convention room to check out the Dark Horse Comic booth, unfortunately after being stopped for the tenth time for pictures, he had given up.

He smiled inwardly as he wove expertly through the crowd heading towards the hallway, where most of the better costumed super fans congregated. His height gave him a slight advantage, at six foot one inches tall he could see over the heads of most people present. This allowed Dillon to find the easiest route through the crowd.

The hallway allowed them to mingle, and kept the congestion away from the vendor area. Anyone could stop and take pictures of all the costumes they wanted, without interfering or causing a traffic snarl. Most years on Saturdays he spent the entire day in the hallway. Fridays he scoped the con out, Saturdays he wore whatever costume he'd come up with for the year and Sunday he spent all his money in the vendor area.

Dillon allowed himself an internal smile of pure contentment; he loved being surrounded by his people. Rather than annoy him, the photo taking gave him a great sense of pride. It meant he'd done his job, if the average con goer recognized him and that they wanted to take his picture. One didn't come to fan expo dressed in costume and not want their photo taken. Dillon was no different, in that way, from any other fan.

"Hey! Great costume. That is so awesome!" A young voice sounded from behind him. "Can I get a picture?"

"Sure." Dillon turned to face a long haired Treky, recognized from his red *Star Trek* uniform. "Your costume looks great too."

"Yours is better." The Treky grinned.

Swirling his cape behind him, Dillon struck a classic pose. The iPhone flashed and the fan turned away with a quick, "Thanks."

Before Dillon could walk away a number of others, young and old, had stopped with their cameras and were taking his picture. He held the pose for a while longer, and then moved on, before he caused another traffic jam.

He walked the rest of the way to the corridor with purpose, his mind on other things. He loved Fan Expo; he'd been coming for six years now. He'd watched the con grow from one small room and about one thousand attendees, to what he saw today. The entire international trade center set aside for nearly forty thousand fans to swarm, over three action filled days.

For the first five years he had come to the con it had been as simple as putting on his costume and catching the subway. That was one of the few perks of living in Toronto. Now that he'd moved back to his home town, negotiating the con had become trickier. He had rented a hotel room and drove in yesterday. Not as convenient, but the benefits of not living in the city far outweighed the negatives as far as Dillon was concerned.

His exit from Toronto last March had come as a surprise to very few people. After the fiasco with Becky, he just couldn't find a reason to stay. The high housing prices? The noise? The traffic jams? The crime rates? No thank you. He'd been eager when his best friend from high school had found him a great house in the town where he'd grown up. Working from home had to have its bonuses, one being that his home could be wherever he wanted. Dillon had spent the last six months fixing the place up; it was a rare but welcome opportunity to work with his hands. His weekends had been spent blissfully covered in drywall dust, as he made the place over into his dream.

Rounding a corner Dillon finally exited the convention room into the hallway, a space fifty feet wide and hundreds of feet long, with escalators anchoring both ends. The ceilings were twenty feet tall and the fluorescent lighting not the best. There were rare benches along the walls but most people grabbed a piece of carpet wherever they could. This space also teemed with people bustling around, in and out of the assorted meeting rooms, posing for pictures and laughing with friends.

"Dillon! Is that you?"

He turned and caught the hand of Ben, who this year had dressed as a Hobbit. They had met the first year of the convention and had seen each other every year since. Dillon wouldn't consider him a 'friend' outside of the con and Facebook, but he seemed like a nice enough guy. His costume choices were prime; Ben had been Darth Vader, Bleach, Superman and Thor. While he may not have fit the costumes the best, being a little on the pudgy side, Ben had so much joy while dressed up that Dillon couldn't fault him. He was a geek to the core and they got along great when they saw one another.

"Ben. Good to see you. Love the costume."

"Thanks. I wish the feet had turned out better." Dillon glanced down at the paper mache feet that Ben wore; they were nearly eighteen inches long and painted realistically. "But hey, they're better than I expected for my first try."

"No, they look good." Dillon assured him.

Ben shrugged. "I see you pulled out old faithful." He motioned towards Dillons costume. "This is what, your fourth year wearing that?"

"Third. But it is my last. I've got some time on my hands so I'll be working on something different for next year."

"Cool. Any spoilers?" Ben arched a scruffy fake eyebrow at him.

"Nah, I'm still at the thinking stage."

"I'm sure you'll come up with something awesome." Dillon just nodded as Ben continued. "If it's your last year, you should definitely check out Catwoman."

Dillon looked at Ben in silent question.

"Catwoman, she's down the hall by the north escalator. Her costume looks as good as yours. That, and she's freaking hot!" Ben waved a hand indicating where he'd seen her previously.

"I think I will. Are you going to the party tonight?"

"You know it." Ben started backing away. "Will I see you there?"

"That's the plan. Later." Dillon gave a short wave and moved towards the north escalator.

As he walked people stopped him a few more times for photo ops. One adorable little boy who Dillon guessed to be approximately five years old had wanted his picture taken with Batman. He knelt beside him for the picture and gave the boy a high five before continuing on his way. He loved this aspect of con, the comradery, the fellowship and, making people happy. It thrilled Dillon when kids wanted their picture taken with him, gauging his costumes success by their reaction to him and what a blast they had when talking with their favorite superheroes.

He smiled slightly as he approached a knot of people, looking over their heads he got his first look at the best Catwoman he'd seen in years. The costume itself was phenomenal, sewn for her perfectly, her body seemed a little curvier than Michelle Pfeiffer's but damn she made PVC look good. She had curves in all the right places and the PVC costume hugged her to perfection. He crossed his arms over his chest and waited.

Catwoman snarled for the camera, crouched near the ground with one leg extended straight out beside her and one hand anchoring her. Her other hand held a bull whip like she knew what to do with it. Flashes flared around the group.

After a moment, bright blue eyes looked up and caught his in a snare that he couldn't look away from. With a tiger like grace Catwoman stood and sauntered through the crowd towards him, the whip trailing on the carpet behind her.

"Well." She purred, her voice low and sexy causing electric sparks to twist up Dillons spine. "What do we have here?" Her tongue darted out over impossibly red lips. "Did you come over here to play with little old me?"

Holding onto his persona became difficult for Dillon as her body swayed near his, and a smell of spicy cinnamon wafted from her. The outfit had definitely been made for her frame, his breath stalled as she sashayed closer still, and Dillon took a moment to thank the costume Gods that his outfit was made of form fitting, inflexible pleather, otherwise he would definitely be showing some wood right now. Her fingers trailed lightly across his chest as she circled around him.

"So, did you come to take me in, Batman?" She purred from behind him.

"Catwoman." Dillon growled, waiting for her to finish her circle. When she stood in front of him once more he said. "Up to your usual kittenish behavior I see."

"Meow." She said, her glistening red lips twitching with suppressed laughter.

"Perhaps I should call the Commissioner?" He let his eyes twinkle at her, but kept his mouth fierce, as per the Batman character.

He leaned towards her, breathing in her heady scent, and whispered. "That costume fits great. It looks authentic."

"Thanks, my sister made it for me. Yours looks amazing too. And thanks for playing along." Her eyes were impossibly blue surrounded by the heavy black makeup.

"Anytime." Dillon murmured. "Do you mind if I hang out here and we let them take some pictures?"

She nodded imperceptibly. Just before pulling away Dillon whispered. "You certainly seem at home as Catwoman."

Her eyes met his with a smile. "You know it."

They both laughed and then posed for pictures.

Chapter 2

The crowds had started to thin and Alora could finally take a breath. She absentmindedly fanned her face, hoping the makeup had stayed in place in the hot hallway. She could feel the perspiration dripping down her spine in an uncomfortable way.

Batman stood right beside her, which didn't help with her overheating. She'd never met a man that caused her this much distraction, this much lust before. And she hadn't even seen his face.

At first she'd thought the costume had to be padded to give all the muscles the proper definition but no, as the day had gone on, she'd discovered it was one hundred percent real. The thin matte pleather formed to Batmans chest in a way that made Aloras breath hitch.

"Excuse me," a voice asked, "could I get your picture?"

"Sure." Alora smiled and began to pose again.

"Batman, will you be in this too?" The teenager, about fifteen, wore some anime costume that Alora didn't understand. It looked good on her, but Alora had no idea what the original character had looked like.

"Love to." Batman's low, gravelly voice sent shivers through Alora as he moved beside her to set up his pose.

Alora, ignored the inner voice that screamed about how impossibly hot Batman's body was, moved into place beside the scrumptious creature. Her body turned towards his, one hand on a rock hard arm while the other trailed the whip in front of them. She turned her face to the camera and pulled her lips into a snarl.

The flash went off at the same time as her libido started thrumming. Started? Who was she kidding; her libido had been in overdrive since Batman first approached. The man smelled like spicy musk mixed with a masculine scent that invaded her brains and sent her on a path of very inappropriate fantasies.

At first she'd worried that the masked fan was a teenager and she looked like a cougar hanging all over him. Being twenty eight she was terrified of finding a buff fourteen year old, complete with a face riddled with acne, beneath the mask. But when she looked up at his tall frame she could see the five o'clock shadow, which assured her of his age appropriateness.

The costume he wore fit stunningly well, it molded to his body in ways that made Aloras eyes cross with lust. Made from black pleather with a long black cape on the back, he looked every bit the part of Batman. Artists would cry over his jawline, for the absolute manly perfection that is projected. She'd found herself wishing the cape would disappear, that way she could see if his rear end lived up to the rest of him.

They'd spent the last four hours posing and chatting amiably with other fans. Batman seemed like a genuinely sweet guy, as he answered questions with a patience that Alora found enviable. He chatted with kids and adults alike and seemed to know quite a few of the other dressed up fans.

She had overheard him telling one lady that he'd had help with the necessary sewing but he had designed the costume himself. She spent some time agonizing over what his face looked like underneath the mask, but his voice had quickly become the sexiest thing she'd heard outside of a television show in years, maybe ever.

A young girl approached her as the day wrapped up. "That is the most amazing costume. But, how do you...I mean, I, how," She stuttered then blurted out. "How do you pee?"

"Carefully." Alora laughed, and then whispered conspiratorially. "Seriously though, easier than one would think. It's actually made in two pieces and I have a side zipper." She pointed to her hip where a hidden zipper had been placed just for those necessary functions.

"Oh. Good thinking." The girl backed away as a few more fans lined up to snap some last minute pics. "Thanks for answering." She laughed and walked away.

Over the loud speakers a voice announced that the hall would close in five minutes and that patrons should begin moving towards the exits.

Alora moved back into another shot with a slight smile, she shivered as Batman's breath slid down her overheated cheek as he posed behind her for more photos. As she looked to the next camera he whispered.

"So, Catwoman. You have me under your spell."

Alora snorted. "Yeah right. But thanks for the compliment."

"You don't believe me?" His full lips twitched as his gravelly voice reached Alora's ears in a soft caress. "Perhaps I should prove it."

He took a half step closer, forcing Alora to look up the entire height of him, her mouth suddenly dry.

"Now, now there are children present." She murmured, trying to stop her heart from beating loud enough for the entire hall to hear.

A scowl crossed his face briefly before his eyes scorched her again and he whispered. "I should make sure you're not one of the kids? You are of legal age?" Alora nodded. "Good. Are you going to the costume party tonight, at Dragonspur?"

Alora nodded again, trying to formulate words in her hormone overloaded brain.

"I guess I'll see you there." With a smile Batman strode away and Alora realized she didn't even know his real name.

She exited the convention center with a satisfied smile on her lips, excited about the upcoming party, determined more than ever to let loose. She'd never had the opportunity nor the urging to have a one-night stand – but tonight could be the night. *"No."* She thought. *"Tonight is the night."* Here, in Toronto, surrounded by people who understood her and her inner geek, she could let go.

***

Three and a half hours later, ten o'clock neared and Alora still hadn't seen Batman anywhere. She had bolstered her failing courage with alcohol while she chatted with a man dressed in full steampunk regalia named Rex, and his friend Jack who had gone full gore with a zombie makeup. Rex's monocle made his dark brown eyes look larger and more intense. The brown leather outfit molded a pretty fine body, to say nothing about the hip hugging gun holster.

"So my dear Catwoman, would you care for another drink?" He smiled, his teeth shining brightly in the dim light of the club.

Alora nodded happily. "A tootsie roll would be great."

"Remind me again, what's in such a girly drink?" Rex laughed.

"A shot of vodka, a shot of crème de cacao and fill 'er with orange juice." Alora said. The tootsie roll had always been her favorite drink.

"And may I ask," Rex smiled, "how many of those concoctions you've had tonight?"

"I," Alora paused in thought, "I, think I've had four or five. Okay maybe six." They were just so delicious; they tasted like candy and went down so easily.

"Your wish, my command." Rex saluted her jauntily.

She felt no pain as he stood and swept across the room to the bar. She had talked to a number of costumed fans since arriving, had danced to Nine Inch Nails and generally had a blast. Alora loved playing the part of social butterfly, in her normal life it stretched pretty far from every day for her.

She looked around taking in the sights of her first real trip to a big city bar. The Dragonspur was a large club filled to capacity with a multitude of costumed geeks. They danced on the strobe light filled dance floor, or chatted at tables around the room. There were little alcoves affording privacy scattered along the walls.

The bar itself dominated the middle of the space; it looked like it had been carved from blackened stone. The most awe inspiring thing about the Dragonspur hovered above the bar. The Dragon sculpture stretched and curled its way across the ceiling, almost twenty five feet in length. The gold and red paint glittered in the dim bar and its eyes glowed with built in lights.

She turned back to the table and Jack smiled at her, a slightly disturbing sight, being that half his face appeared to be blown off due to his zombie makeup. "Catwoman. You are one amazing looking woman."

Alora laughed, the world tilting around her a little. "You can't see my face zombie Jack, how do you know?"

"Trust me, I can tell." Jacks eyes gleamed as he took a swig of his Budweiser.

Her chair jostled from behind as Rex returned and she jumped slightly in shock. "I took the liberty and got several drinks. That way we don't have to fight to get to the bar later." He set a tray down on their table which already overflowed with drinks, shots and empty glasses.

"First shot goes to the lovely lady." Rex handed Alora a shot glass filled with some sort of red liquid. She wasn't a stranger to alcohol but it had been a while since she'd had this much in such a short span of time.

"Thanks." She took the shot, and fiery liquid burned its way down her throat.

***

Dillon cursed inwardly as the cab finally pulled up outside of the Dragonspur. The clock showed nearly eleven; he had intended to be here at nine.

"That'll be twenty two dollars." The cabbie, a middle aged man with graying hair and a mischievous smile said.

Dillon handed over the cash and went to get out of the yellow vehicle as the cab driver laughed and added. "Guess the Batmobiles in the shop, huh?'

"Alfreds having it detailed." Dillon shot back and got out of the cab with a laugh. He walked up to the building and allowed the sounds of music and people to overwhelm him as he entered.

He was late because of his ex-girlfriend. Well, he had been running late and then his ex had made him even later. Becky had somehow figured out that he had come into the city for the weekend and caught him unprepared on the phone as he had gotten out of the shower. Dillon replayed the conversation in his mind as he scanned the bar.

"Dillon, I heard you were in town. Why didn't you call me?' Becky had opened the conversation with.

"Becky. I didn't call because we broke up."

A silence that Dillon understood only too well had followed. Endeavoring to be polite he had asked. "How are you?"

"I'm good. I've wanted to call you." Becky's voice had murmured softly. "I missed you."

"Becky." Dillon's voice was wary, unsure of the direction of the conversation.

"What? I thought we had a good thing going."

"We fought all the time. It wasn't a good thing Becky. The time had come for both of us to move on." Dillon fought to keep exasperation from his voice.

For two years he and Becky had lived together, Dillon had gone into the relationship expecting it to be a lifetime commitment. Becky was a beautiful woman, tall, blonde and willowy, everything he thought he wanted. Her modeling career had just started to take off when they had met at a launch party for the software Dillon had just finished. They had hit it off immediately. In the beginning Becky had claimed to love gaming and spent days just playing and watching movies with Dillon.

Unfortunately it turned out Becky had just faked an interest to be with him: she liked to party and spent as much time as she could at various clubs which just bored Dillon. He had made efforts to fit in with her world, but he didn't belong. Dillon spent all his time working or playing games which drove Becky up the wall.

The last six months of their relationship had been torturous. Dillon had discovered Becky had been shoring up her modeling assets with his money. She didn't make enough to cover for the costs of new photos for her portfolio and needed cash to cover other expenses. Normally Dillon wouldn't have minded, but when he paid all the household expenses and then also ended up forking out money so Becky could schmooze with fashion designers and agencies, it got to be too much. They had argued that Becky needed to get a job to cover at least the cost of her networking and she had lost it.

It got to the point where Dillon knew he had to get out. He'd been as kind as possible, giving up his apartment, moving out of town, and he'd even given her a generous settlement. He felt in his heart the relationship wasn't right for either of them, he knew there had to be someone better for him.

"I was wrong. I've wanted to call and tell you that, but I've been a chicken. Then when I heard you were in town I knew it I had to do it now. Maybe you were right and the time had come to move on," Becky had whispered with tears in her voice, "but what we had was special, it will always be special to me."

"I think you may be remembering something different. It was good while it lasted but, we had our problems. A lot of them, and that's why we aren't together anymore."

A sniffle from the other end had Dillon rolling his eyes; she could turn on the waterworks at whim. "But the sex was fantastic, wasn't it?" She asked.

"It was good." *When you weren't preserving your face, too tired, couldn't have bags under your eyes or were actually home.*

"Yeah." Becky sighed, obviously remembering something completely different from Dillon.

"So," she asked softly, "are you seeing anyone?"

"No. You?"

"I am. His name is Palo, he's a fashion photographer. We are really good together. In ways you and I never were." Her soft tone belied a happiness and bitterness rolled into one.

"Honestly Becky, I'm happy for you. I knew when I left that it wasn't right and that I had to leave or get lost in the everyday of us. I didn't break up with you to hurt you; I did it because I thought it needed to happen."

"So why haven't you called, I thought you wanted to be friends?"

"I do. I guess I haven't because I needed the distance that time would bring. And you were so mad when I left that I couldn't be sure if you would even take my call."

"I understand. I said some very hurtful things. I wanted to apologize, and to say, thank you. You made the right choice."

And so the conversation had gone. It took Dillon almost an hour to get her off the phone, now he wanted nothing more than a stiff drink to celebrate. He hadn't realized how torn up he had still been over hurting Becky. Her tear stained, screaming face had haunted him ever since he had left. The conversation tonight had brought closure to both of them and filled Dillon with a relief he hadn't known he needed.

Dillon negotiated the crowd like a pro as he made his way to the bar and ordered a rye and coke. His eyes scanned the crowd, looking over costumes in a detached manner. Really he knew he kidded himself, he wanted to find Catwoman.

All day he'd stayed by her side, with her spicy sweet smell in his nostrils and her gentle laugh filling his ears as she talked to fans. A few times he'd wanted to shoot the crowds taking their pictures, just to get some time to talk to her. But he'd held his composure, waiting for his chance when they weren't surrounded by geeked out comic addicts. He hoped she hadn't already left so they could actually talk and see if they got along with more than their choice of DC characters, that and maybe get each other's actual names.

He looked at the dance floor, smiling as he caught Rick from *The Walking Dead* dirty dancing with Princess Leia to the tempo filled song Tainted Love by Softcell. A mass of bodies moved in tandem to the music surrounding them as they hid in their own world.

Frustrated at not seeing her immediately, Dillon took his drink and began to wander the room, eyes on the lookout for the enchanting Catwoman; he caught tidbits of conversations as he went.

"Halo is the best first person shooter game…"

"Who would win in a fight between The Hulk and Spiderman?"

"The tenth Doctor was the best!"

"Wizards of the coast have done a rocking job with DND."

"Are you kidding me? Third edition was a complete sell out!"

Dillon let the buzz of conversations beat around him, paying little heed to the raised, excited voices. As he slipped past the dance floor his eyes were snared by the vision he had hoped for.

Catwoman. Her head tilted back in a laugh as she sat at a low table, facing him, while two men sat with their backs to the room. Dillon moved towards her with purpose, intent on buying her a drink, chatting with her, seeing her, smelling her, being near her, anything.

He moved closer and noticed she seemed to be swaying in her chair, her eyes half closed. One of the men handed her a shot glass as Dillon got close enough to hear.

"Another shot, you can't say no! I bought these just for you."

Catwoman shook her head slightly. She slurred, "I don' thin' I shuld. Can't do no more shots."

"Just one more." The guy wheedled. "It's rude to say no when someone has bought you drinks." He leaned over the table and held the glass to Catwoman's lips. His hand caressed her arm in a blatantly seductive move.

Catwoman closed her eyes and allowed the shot to be poured down her throat. She sputtered, rubbing the back of her hand over her face and smearing her bright red lipstick slightly. "No more." Her head leaned towards the table, intoxicated.

Dillon moved up just as the guy offered her the last shot. Steampunk ran a finger down her cheek in a way that set Dillon's stomach on fire. The sleazy guy had the nerve to touch her, and ply an obviously drunk girl with alcohol. Dillon felt an overpowering urge to protect this tiny woman.

A glove encased hand cupped the back of Catwoman's head, "This is the last shot. After its gone you're done." He waved a hand towards the table liberally littered with empty glasses. "See. The last one."

Catwoman continued to feebly shake her head. Dillon read her lips as she whispered, "No more."

"Come on baby, this is the last one. Then we can go dance." He held the drink to her lips, and Dillon stepped up, anger heating his eyes.

"The lady said no."

The steampunk guy looked up. "This is none of your business Batman." He nodded towards his zombie friend. "Catwoman is with us. Go find your own chick."

Dillon shook his head. "Unless you want the bouncer coming over I would suggest you walk away now."

"Come on man." Steampunk guy whined. "We've already spent a chunk of change on this chick and she's just about to finish up the last drink." He held the shot glass back to Catwoman's lips.

"As I said." Dillon gritted his teeth the muscles, in his jaw twitching. "She said no." Dillon reached out a hand and snatched the shot glass from steampunks hand. "I think you should be going. I'll take care of her."

Catwoman looked up through almost closed eyes. "Batman! You came. I was jus' waitin' fer you. Rex an' Jack were jus' keepin' me company."

Steampunk looked like he wanted to continue to argue, but he dropped his hands from Catwoman at a wave from his zombie friend.

"Fine. We're going. There are plenty of pussies around here." The two men stood and weaved their way towards the bar.

Dillon moved closer to Catwoman as she listed forward on the table. He put his arm around her waist and moved them to one of the quieter alcoves, practically carrying her. As they moved across the club he motioned to a passing waitress that he needed water for her.

He pushed her gently onto the bench seat and maneuvered himself across the table.

"Hey. Are you okay?"

Her head bobbed up towards him. "I's ok. Jus' a li'l drunk." She held her finger and thumb almost together to indicate just how drunk she thought she was.

The quick waitress showed up with a large glass of water. She eyed Catwoman warily, "She can't puke in here. If she's that drunk she needs to go home."

"Not gonna puke." Catwoman muttered. "Ne'er puke. Too messy. I be fine." She nodded emphatically, her entire body moving with the motion.

Dillon turned to the pretty woman with a reassuring smile. "I've got her. Don't worry. She won't throw up."

The waitress looked like she didn't believe him but moved away anyways.

"Okay, drunken kitty cat, I need you to drink some water. Then I will get you home."

Catwoman sipped at the water then shook her head, "Not goin' home. Hotel."

"Okay. I'll get you to the hotel." The feeling of protection that had overcome Dillon when he saw the bawdry guys trying to pick her up still overwhelmed him when he looked into her beautiful, but drunken eyes.

"Tanks." Catwoman took another drink of water. "You very hawt, ya know."

Dillon laughed. "Have some more water, and then we'll get you a cab. Where is your room key?"

Catwoman reached into her elbow high glove and fumbled as she pulled out a plastic room key that she handed to Dillon with a guileless smile. He glanced at it long enough to note the Royal York hotel emblem, with room 326 noted on the white surface.

"You gonna stay wif me?" She asked shyly.

"I will get you to your room safely." Dillon assured her.

"D'ya wanna have shex wif me?" Her eyes were bloodshot as she asked.

Dillon groaned. "Yes. But not when you're this drunk."

"Oh." She looked down, and then took another drink of water. "I wanded to ha' shex wif you."

"Another time, kitty cat. I don't take advantage of drunken women." Dillon reached out a hand to steady Catwoman.

"I's not tha' drunk. I can have shex." Kitty retorted with a gleam in her eyes that in any other instance Dillon would have been thrilled to explore.

"Another time." He said regretfully.

"Shuch a gennleman." She muttered with a laugh. "Wish I knew mor' gennlemen."

She looked introspective for a moment before she started talking. Dillon leaned closer to hear what Catwoman said.

"Stupid ex. Why do men suck so mush? I just wanna do my thin' an' he got me 'victed. I gotta move. Can't tell m'famly. Can't tell no one. All m'money gone to lawyer an' damn lawyer din't do nufin'. You no' a lawyer are ya?" She looked up at Dillon questioningly.

"No, kitty, I am definitely not a lawyer."

"Good. Cuz lawyers suck."

"So your ex got you evicted from your home?" He asked gently, to which she nodded. "And your lawyer took all your money." She nodded again and wiped at a single tear that slipped from her eye.

"E'en money not mine. Took commishion fer a sculpture ha' ta use tha' money ta pay lawyers. Now I don' ha' no studio. I's screwed."

She looked away, distracted momentarily by a shiny Silver Surfer costume that walked by. She swung her head back towards Dillon and continued.

"Gotta make sculpture. Nowhere ta make it. No place ta live. No place to work. I's screwed." Her voice got louder in drunken indignation. "An' HE said I suckt in bed, tha's why he cheated on me, wif a twenty year ol' bimbo."

"Your boyfriend cheated on you?" Dillon asked calmly as he reached for her hand in an effort to comfort her.

"Husban' and ya, I did ever'thing for him. Twied ta be da perfec' wife, it didn' matter. Not at all. I's alone. Two years, alone." She swung her hand holding up two fingers and nearly knocked the glass from the table before Dillon caught it and handed it to her.

"That sucks kitty, I'm sorry."

"Is ok. I foun' m'callin', love sculpting. Thash da good thin' but he screwt me again." She fell silent and closed her pain filled eyes.

"Catwoman." Her eyes opened slowly and looked blurrily at him. "Are you alone tonight?"

"Naah. M'sista stayin' wif me a'the hotel." Her head bobbed dangerously towards the table.

"Is your sister here?" He asked, looking around.

Catwoman shook her head negative. "She's at 'nother party."

Dillon felt a stab of relief that at least she wouldn't be alone all night, then he sighed, the woman had some obvious pain and had started to bottom out from the drinking. She'd finished her water, so he helped her up and worked them through the throng of people to the door.

Outside the cooler air seemed to momentarily revitalize Catwoman and she managed to stand somewhat on her own while Dillon hailed a cab for them. He deposited her in the backseat, climbed in beside her and gave the cabbie the destination.

While the vehicle whirled through the city Catwoman rested her head on Dillons shoulder and whispered. "Sorry ta be drun' and whiny. Tanks for takin' care o'me." Before she closed her eyes and passed out.

The warmth of her body against his kept Dillon focused. Frustration filled him that she'd gotten this drunk and that they hadn't been able to have a real conversation, though he felt a kinship and compassion for the woman whose life appeared to be falling apart.

Sooner than expected the cab pulled up in front of the hotel Catwoman was staying at. Dillon paid the driver and made an effort to awaken the woman beside him. After a few attempts which roused little more than groans Dillon sighed and picked her up.

He quickly made his way through the, thankfully empty lobby and hitched the elevator up to the third floor. After fumbling with the keycard while still carrying Catwoman, Dillon finally managed to open the door and flip on a light. He set her on the nearest bed as she curled up onto her side. Then deciding she couldn't be comfortable he removed the hooker boots she wore and set them beside the bed. He reached the laces holding her mask on and deftly undid them, tossing the mask on the night stand.

White blond hair with stunning bright blue tips spilt out over his fingers. He brushed it back from her face as she sighed in her sleep and turned towards him.

Dillons hands stilled with shock as he looked into the face of Alora Mcintosh. Her hair might be different but this face had haunted his dreams for a long time. The wide blue eyes, the full lips, pert little nose and small scar above her left eyebrow, that was all Alora. He would know her anywhere. He hadn't seen her in ten years; a face from his past, his high school sweetheart, the girl who had broken his heart.

Chapter 3

Alora dug her fingers deep in the clay, lost in thought. Her strong, skilled hands molded and kneaded fresh chunks of the wet muddy substance to even out the moisture. She didn't have to think at this stage just let muscle memory take over. Piece by piece she grabbed and worked, until she set it aside and pulled more from the bag.

While this mind numbing activity took place Alora allowed her thoughts to wander. It had been a week since she got home from Fan Expo. She had gone to the convention center on the Sunday, hung over but unwilling to miss the last day, and hoping for a glimpse of Batman.

She had vague memories of the costume party, she remembered Batman being there and the steampunk guy and the zombie. But what they talked about she had no idea, nor did she know how she got back to her room.

When she had awoken on Sunday morning, with a pounding head and a vow to never drink again, there had been a note left on the bedside table for Cass.

I brought her back to the hotel, Catwoman got a little drunk. Take care of her.

Batman

So she'd gone to the exhibition and wandered around, wanting to at least thank him for taking care of her, but to no avail. She had been unsuccessful in her attempts to find her dark hero.

Since she'd been home Alora had been trying to figure out a way out of the mess she found herself in. Her eviction notice said she had a week; she had packed up her personal belongings but had no place to take them. All the furniture belonged to the house so at least she had very little to move.

The only room in the small house not packed was her studio. A dark little room in the basement filled with clay, tools, a small kiln and her beat up work surface. She sat on the stool today praying for a revelation. To somehow know what to do.

Last week she had taken her resume all over town, no one was hiring. Or at least no one would hire a twenty eight year old woman who hadn't worked in ten years. She had no money for last month's rent and no job, so potential landlords were unwilling to take a risk on her, and really she couldn't blame them. She had taken all her existing pieces and sold some of the more conventional ones at the farmers market, but it wasn't nearly enough.

She cursed Wendell again for being such an ass. Their entire married life she had spent at home like he wanted, taking care of him. She had been the perfect little wife to the big accountant. Now that he left her, she had no life skills, and no way to gain any.

In the two years since their break up she had started sculpting again and found the passion she had thought lost in high school. She had also discovered a real talent that she had suppressed more than she expected.

They had fought with lawyers, and Alora had lost the battle. More than that she had lost the war. The courts had decided that she didn't deserve the house she'd called home, a portion of his pension, nothing. The half of their savings that she had been awarded had already been eaten up with frivolous things like food and rent.

Then, two months ago she found out Wendell had talked to her landlord about her 'unsteady influence' and a bunch of other crap, so now she found herself being evicted. It was an old boys club and Wendell knew all the old boys to talk to.

Her Mom had always loved Aloras art and had taken her portfolio to the bank where she worked. They had contracted Alora to do a sizeable sculpture, for the foyer, and paid her a good chunk of moolah as a commission to get the piece done. That money had gone to pay the lawyer and now she had less than sixty days to finish the piece and nowhere to do it. If she defaulted, or couldn't complete the sculpture not only did it reflect badly on her Mom, but she'd have to give the down payment back.

In short she was screwed.

The front door to the house banged open, pulling Alora from her dark thoughts.

"Hey! It's Cass and Brant."

"I'm in the studio. I'm covered in muck; I'll be right up." Alora yelled back.

Footsteps stomped loudly down the stairs ignoring her. Then two figures appeared in the doorway. Brant came in first, followed by Cass. The room suddenly seemed crowded.

"Hey. Whatcha working on?" Brant looked at the table curiously.

"Right now nothing. Just prepping the clay for sculpting." Alora said as she looked at her twin. Brant and her couldn't be much different. He stood nearly six inches taller, and had dark brown hair kept in a short buzz cut. His eyes were brown and crinkled when he laughed. As much as it nastied her out she knew her twin was a hottie. Much sought after by the girls in town. His tall body stayed muscular and fit; he took his job as a firefighter seriously and worked out every day to maintain his form.

Realizing she had been wool gathering she grabbed a plastic sheet and threw it over the clay. "Let me just wash up and then we can talk, I can get you something to drink."

She turned to the sink, hoping she still had some coffee left upstairs to make for them. Taking a moment to clean her hands in the small work sink she turned her head.

"What brings both of you by?"

"We wanted to talk to you." Cass said in an unusually serious voice.

"Shit. That doesn't sound good. Did I do something wrong?" She turned back, but both of them had unreadable expressions on their faces. "Okay. You're freaking me out." She dried her hands. "Let's go upstairs and sit down."

After everyone had settled in the living room, Brant and Cass sat on the faded couch facing Alora on the beat up lazy boy chair, Alora began to get concerned. "Is something wrong? Mom and Dad? Daxia, Eric? Is everyone okay?"

"They're all fine." Cass stated. "That's not why we're here." Alora breathed a sigh of relief at least nothing had gone wrong with her family.

"We're here about you." Brant's low voice rumbled across the room.

"Me? Why?" Alora leaned back and took up a defensive position, her arms crossed over her chest.

"Come on Alora. Why aren't you talking to us?" Cass huffed.

"Talking to you about what?" Alora evaded answering the question.

"Okay fine, you want blunt. I'll be blunt." Brant leaned forward as he spoke, his brown eyes glittering. "Why is your house packed up? You haven't told us where you're moving or why. Your kitchen is virtually empty. Cass noticed you didn't eat anything that cost more than ten bucks while you were in Toronto. Are you having financial troubles? For Christ sakes, why the hell did I have to hear from Chief Tanner that you were being evicted?"

"Chief Tanner? What? Why?" She sputtered.

"He knows your landlord and asked if I needed time off to help you move. Imagine how stupid I felt when I had no idea you were even moving!"

"And I," Cass started, "got reamed out by this jackass. He assumed I knew all about it and had kept your secret. I had to beat into him that I had been left in the dark too." She waved a hand at Brant. "Dammit Alora, we're family. Why aren't you talking to us?"

Alora hung her head. "Fine. I didn't talk to you guys, or anyone, because there's nothing anyone can do. I have to figure this shit out myself."

"Maybe we can't do anything but you are acting like you're all alone. You aren't confiding in us. Maybe we could help you find a solution. Or something." Cass's exasperated voice exploded.

"I didn't want to burden anyone." Alora whispered.

"Screw that. We're your family; you're supposed to burden us." Brant stated. "So talk."

Alora organized her thoughts for a minute before she started. She looked at the carpet not wanting to see the disappointment in her siblings' eyes. "I ran into trouble. Wendell apparently bad mouthed me to the landlord and now I've been evicted. I have to move out next week, I don't have a job, so no one will rent me a place. I have nowhere to go, and the down payment the bank gave me for the sculpture went to pay my divorce lawyer so I didn't go into collections."

"Is the sculpture done?" Cass asked quietly to which Alora shook her head and said.

"No. My studio here isn't big enough to do the piece. And I can't start it with having to move. I know what I plan on doing, I just can't begin yet, but I only have sixty days to get it made and bronzed before I default on that too."

"Have you tried to get a job?" Brant asked.

"Of course, that was my first step. No one is hiring, and even if they were I don't have any recent or relevant experience. I've even tried Tim Horton's to no luck."

"Shit." Both Cass and Brant muttered.

"I know. I've been trying to find work for the last while, there's just nothing. That's why I was so thrilled with the commission from the bank, but it doesn't look like that is going to work out either."

"What about the divorce stuff? Shouldn't you be getting a chunk of change from that?" Brant's eyes lit up, and then faded quickly as Alora shook her head.

"Nope. Apparently I only get half the savings account, which went to pay for rent and stuff over the last few years. The house, the car everything goes to Wendell and his new bimbo."

"That's bullshit." Cass yelped. "You don't get anything? You gave ten years of your life to that sad pissflap and you get nothing!"

"Unfortunately yes. Wendells lawyers had a field day with the fact that I 'lazed around at home' while he worked his ass off to support me. If we had of had kids," she winced, "it might have turned out different. But the courts didn't seem to believe that it was his idea for me to stay home."

"Did you tell them about the miscarriage? And why you miscarried?" Brant shot out.

"I did. They didn't believe me; in their minds he could do no wrong. Wendell's lawyers were better than mine. I just have to start over from zero." Alora sighed.

"I wish you had of let me go after that rat bastard." Brant's fury filled voice showed his frustration and anger.

"Really Brant? And how exactly would that have helped anything? Besides ruining your chances to be a firefighter. It wouldn't have done anything." Alora allowed her voice to be harsh.

"I would have at least felt better. You are much too good for that piece of shit." Alora shrugged at her brothers' response.

"Listen guys, I know you mean well, but there's not much you can do." Alora's defeated voice said. "I can't move in with either of you. Brant you're in a house with six other guys, I can't move in there, you have no room. Cass you're just starting out, in that tiny apartment and all your extra space is covered in fabrics. I can't do it. I won't do it."

"How about a loan?" Brant asked.

"No. The bank turned me down, I have no way to pay them back and no credit rating. I won't borrow money from you or anyone else." Aloras pride reared its head and she snapped. "I am an adult, I got myself into this mess, and I will find a way out."

Cass and Brant held up their hands defensively. "Wooah." Cass said. "Have you talked to Mom and Dad? They would let you move back home, or front you the cash you need."

"Of course they would. But it's wrong to even ask. Both Daxia and Eric are going to be in university this year. What with Dad getting laid off last year, they're in a tight financial situation as is. I know they would take me in without question, but I want to find a solution that doesn't involve me running home like some errant child and besides, there isn't enough room for me to sculpt. Trust me I thought of it. I'm trying to figure out a way to be an adult who doesn't need a husband or her parents. I want to be able to figure it out myself."

"I know you're trying." Brant leaned forward softening his tone. "But, if you need help that's what family is for. I would happily loan you some cash to get you through until the sculpture is done."

"Thanks. I appreciate knowing you would loan me the money. I am gonna check the paper again today. And no worries, if I can't find anything I will move back home, it's just my last choice. I won't be totally homeless."

"Listen, we came over here, intending to get all pissy with you. An intervention you could call it. I get that you're trying to be all mature and stuff but we are here for you. At least use us to blow off steam. We love you and after everything you went through with Wendell you deserve better. We just want to help however we can." Cass' eyes were suspiciously damp.

"I know you guys are here. But everyone is so busy, and I hate asking for help." Alora's eyes teared up a little at the sentiment from her two closest siblings.

"You need to stop this bullshit about not asking for help." Brant said gruffly.

"I AM the oldest." Alora muttered. "I shouldn't need help."

"Oldest by seven minutes doesn't count." Brant smiled.

"It sure as hell does." Alora reiterated the argument they'd had all their lives.

Brant and Alora were born first, followed seventeen months later by Cass. It had always been the three of them together. Daxia came along five years later followed by Eric two years after that. Because of the age differences, the top three, as they referred to themselves, were closer and the youngest two backed each other up.

"Okay." Brant said gruffly, hiding his emotions behind a tough guy exterior as he always did. "Just don't take it all to heart. And remember we are here, even if it's just to vent to. You gotta let loose, things will fall into line."

"So, if you want me to let loose are you finally gonna introduce me to one of those hot firefighters you work with?" Alora teased.

"Yeah! I wouldn't mind a spin down a fine fireman's pole." Cass waggled her eyebrows.

"Ugh." Brant made a choking noise. "I just threw up in my mouth Cass. And that is why I don't introduce either of you to the guys I work with."

A few hours later both her siblings had left and Alora had just finished looking through the paper. There were circles around a number of potential studios, although the higher rent had her clutching her virtual purse strings. She figured she could pull up a chunk of floor and sleep in the studio if need be. Getting somewhere to work far outweighed the need for a proper apartment.

She had called two different landlords and had realized that neither would work for her needs. The phone sat beside her on the beat up table as she girded herself to call the next one on the list.

The doorbell rang saving her for now, and filling Alora with gratitude. She stood up and walked to the front door, knowing it wasn't her family; they just walked in and yelled.

Opening the door she looked up into the face of Dillon Edwards, her high school sweetheart, whom she hadn't seen in ten years.

Shock stalled her tongue. She froze and stared, he looked so different from when they had dated. Gone was the skinny, acne covered geek she had fallen for in her junior year. He had filled out; the t-shirt he wore clung to muscles that were clearly defined. His hair was longer than the military cut she remembered. It now fell in shiny waves to his shoulders, black as sin. She felt an immediate shock of lust, he looked great.

"Alora." He nodded at her in greeting. "Can I come in?"

"Ahh, yeah." Overcoming her shock she shook her head and backed into the living room. "Dillon, it's been a long time. What are you doing in Kennedy?"

She waved him towards the couch in an invitation to sit. Her mind raced; she never thought she'd see Dillon again. Confusion warred inside her, unsure why he had come and what he wanted, Alora tried to calm herself as she sat in the lazy boy.

Dillon moved into the living room and made himself comfortable on the couch. His arm spread along the back of the sofa and an ankle crossed over his knee, he looked relaxed and at home.

"I actually moved back here in March."

"Really? I'm surprised I haven't seen you around." Alora paused, realizing she had hidden out for the last year and avoided being in public. "I was sorry to hear about your Mom. I always remember what a great woman she was."

Mrs. Edwards had passed away the year after Alora had graduated from high school; she had read it in the paper.

Dillon nodded. "Thank you; it's been a long time."

"I thought you were living in Toronto?"

"I was, but my work allows me to live where I want to, and when the opportunity to buy my house came up, I couldn't resist."

"Nice." Alora fell silent, unsure what to say. The quiet ticking of the clock in the kitchen seemed more like a gong as they looked each other over.

"So." Alora started at the same time as Dillon said.

"So."

They laughed lightly and Dillon nodded at Alora indicating she should talk first.

"I guess I'm wondering what brings you to my house today. We haven't seen each other in, like, ten years."

Dillon shook his head. "Actually we saw each other just last week."

Alora tilted her head in question.

"Catwoman." His pearly white smile caused Aloras heart to beat faster.

"You were at Fan Expo?" Her voice trailed off as her brain sluggishly strung the pieces together. "Batman? But, what? But? How?" She stuttered.

Dillon nodded with a grin. Disbelief filled Alora; this was the Batman she had flirted with all day. Her confusion turned to horror as she put two and two together and realized he had gotten her back to her hotel, zambonied out of her mind. She had no idea what she had said or did after a certain point in the night.

Her horror must have shown on her face because Dillon smiled gently and said. "It's okay. You were a bit drunk, but you didn't embarrass yourself too badly."

Alora dropped her face into her hands mumbling. "Too badly. Great. Thanks, that reassures me ever so much."

She could feel her face warm; telling her that redness had flushed her pale cheeks so that she looked as though she had spent a week in Cuba. Nonetheless she looked up at Dillon.

"Thank you for taking care of me. I really don't remember much from the night." She paused. "Okay so we saw each other last week, that still doesn't tell me what you are doing here."

"Well," Dillon drawled, running his thumb over his lower lip in an unconscious move that set Aloras libido on fire. "Here's the thing. When you were…intoxicated, shall we say? You mentioned that you needed a place to stay and a place to work out of." Alora nodded suspiciously. "My house has five bedrooms. I had always intended to rent out at least one of the rooms. I thought perhaps I could help you out."

Alora automatically shook her head. "I don't need charity Dillon."

"It's not charity. You could pay me back rent when you get paid for the sculpture you're working on." Dillon quickly said.

"That's nice and all, but I need a studio space." Alora searched Dillons face trying to figure out where his ulterior motive lay.

"I have a large workshop, separated from the main house, that I think would work perfectly for a studio. It's heated and has both space and light, the previous owner renovated it for a man cave." Dillon smiled. "I could use the money; it would really help me out. I'm not sure how handy you are. I've been working away on the old place, and if you were able to help with some renovations, we could take that off the rent."

"If you need the money, why not rent it to someone who can pay right away?" Alora questioned.

"Because I'm still in mid renovation, I can't rent it out officially to anyone yet." Dillon sighed. "The updating is taking longer than I expected and I am finding myself stretched thin, both on time and energy, and to some degree, money. I can't rent the rooms until the renos are done, but I can't get the renos done until I get help."

"I'm not bad with my hands." Alora thought of all the DIY projects she had completed that Wendell hadn't appreciated over the years. "Nothing too in depth, but your basic work I am quite capable of doing."

"Great!" Dillon grinned happily. "So, it's a deal then?"

He stood up and reached out a hand to shake Aloras. She thought for a moment about her options then took a deep breath and shook his. An electric shock of lust surged through Alora as soon as their fingers touched, and her eyes flew to Dillons just in time to see his darken with desire.

Hold it together woman! She thought half incoherently as she tightened her grip and forcing the English language back onto her tongue, she whispered.

"It's a deal."

***

Dillon managed to not fist pump, and yell an exuberant "Yes!" when Alora agreed to move in with him.

After coming home from Fan Expo, Alora had been at the top of his mind. He had been unable to banish the thoughts of her and her troubles. Finally, after wracking his brains he had come up with a solution that would help Alora out.

He did have the space, and could help her out, so why wouldn't he? Then when he'd seen her again, he felt the purely physical pull from her and it made him more determined than ever.

She looked so different from when they had dated; her hair alone had been a shock. Back then it had been a soft light brown; she had been a very pretty girl in a soft unassuming way. Now with her dyed white blond hair with the brilliant blue tips, she was stunning. A man couldn't look away from the type of woman Alora had become. Her blue eyes shone like they were lit from behind and her fine skin seemed so pale it looked translucent.

Even right now with her hair haphazardly up in a messy bun on top of her head with a smudge of clay on her blushing cheek she looked like a comic character come to life.

He had asked around about this Wendell Blakey she had been married to. The answers were all pretty much the same; the guy was a total asshat. He had screwed around on Alora the entire length of their marriage, or so the rumors went, and left her for some young little bimbette who worked for him. There were also whispers about how he'd treated Alora, but nothing definitive that Dillon could find out.

Shaking the thoughts from his head he turned to Alora and slowly released her hand. "I see you're packed already, did you want to move now? I brought my vehicle so I can give a hand."

Her bright blue eyes looked shocked as she stared up at him. "Uh," she stuttered. "I still have to pack up my studio and a few other things. You don't have to help me move, I can get Brant or my Dad to come over."

"I don't mind." Dillon said easily. "Why don't I come back in a few hours and I can give you a hand then. I'm already free today so rather than bug your brother why don't I just get you moved."

Alora frowned making Dillon ache to kiss the downturned corners of her mouth. "I guess. I'd appreciate the help; I don't have a car right now so I will take advantage of your offer."

"Sounds great." Dillon smiled.

"Why are you doing this Dillon?" She whispered her eyes suspiciously shiny.

"Ah, Kitty, you deserve a break." Dillon couldn't resist, he ran a hand over her cheek gently. Her skin felt like silk under his roughened fingers.

"But why you? You don't owe me anything." She looked up at him, unconsciously rubbing her cheek against the palm of his hand.

"I may not owe you anything but we were once friends weren't we?"

Alora nodded, her eyes closed momentarily as she added, "The best."

"So let's see if we can be friends again." Dillon's low and rough voice betrayed his intensity.

Just touching Alora once made his body tingle with fire. He knew he wanted so much more but he also didn't want to either scare her off, or think too much about what his reasons were. He had felt an overpowering urge to protect her since he first saw her drunk in that skin tight ultra-sexy Catwoman costume. He also knew he hadn't been this attracted to any woman in a long time. His body pulsed and throbbed with pure want. But he also had to take it slow with Alora; she had been the one to end their relationship years ago. He didn't want to get burned again. He slowly pulled away from the temptation in front of him and smiled.

"I'll take off and see you around four, if that's okay with you?"

Alora looked at her cell phone then nodded. "Yeah, four should be fine. Again, thanks a lot Dillon."

Just the way she said his name made him surge with lust. But he fought down his base instincts and replied, "No problem." Before he let himself out the front door and strode to his SUV happily.

He knew from what he'd heard, both in rumor and what he'd established when Alora had been drunk that her marriage hadn't been the greatest. And that she'd had a lot of problems in the last ten years.

His first instinct once he knew Catwoman was Alora had been to run away. She'd hurt him when she dumped him and frankly he wanted none of it. But then he thought about how great they'd gotten along before they broke up and the chemistry he felt with her now. He wanted answers about the past and to help someone who had once meant a great deal to him. This was his chance. A chance to find out what had happened all those years ago and why. A chance to get to know the woman that his first love had become.

He drove across town to his place and pulled into the driveway with a sigh. This home was everything he'd ever wanted. A huge hundred year old red Victorian house, with all the charm and all the problems, had become his dream. The overgrown gardens ran along one side of the semicircular drive and an enormous covered porch flanked the other.

Dillon threw the car into park and went around the main building to the carriage house at the back along the fence line of the property. Using his key he let himself in and took a few moments to tidy the space, making sure any of his belongings were stored in the loft area. He swept the cement floor section and vacuumed the man cave space which overlooked the workshop. That finished and the space looking presentable he relocked the door and popped into the back door of his house.

He took the stairs two at a time and bee lined for the second largest bedroom in the house, which was one that he'd luckily finished last month. Soft yellow walls blended seamlessly with the cream colored carpet and the four poster heavy wooden bed in the middle of the room stood out in a traditional manner. The attached bathroom wasn't refinished yet but it did function, for now it would do. The room faced south west, allowing the best afternoon sunlight to stream in through the multi paned windows.

Dillon quickly emptied the room of the minimal amount of personal items. Then he cracked the window to get some fresh air and went downstairs to wait. Four o'clock seemed very far away.

Chapter 4

Alora cuddled down in the soft comforter, not wanting to get out of bed. Yesterday had been such an upheaval, first with her siblings visit, then with Dillons. He had arrived back at four o'clock and with only three trips (two of which were her studio equipment) she had been ensconced in the stunning house he had bought.

Upon arriving she had dumped her personal stuff in the bedroom and proceeded to spend eight hours in what was now her studio, inside the carriage house at the back of the property. She set everything up perfectly, then sat in the space getting used to it. The studio boasted a kitchenette, a small living area and a two piece bathroom at the back. Old comfortable furniture that had been delegated as not nice enough for the main building had made its way to the carriage house.

The front half of the studio had cement floors and lots of windows where a garage door had once been. The loft area housed Dillon's belongings, but she wouldn't need access to that space, she had more than she'd dared hope for. Alora loved it. It felt lived in and she felt inspired to create here.

She had sat in the studio for hours just sketching and thinking. She had barely turned around and found the clock had miraculously hit three in the morning. Alora couldn't wait to truly begin creating in the sun filled open space. She had slid into bed quietly in the late night, feeling a little out of her element. Even as exhausted as she had been, knowing that Dillon slept just across the hall had made it difficult to fall asleep.

Her thoughts had circled around the fact that he was there, and that he'd gone out of his way to help her when he didn't have to. He had changed from the adorable geek she'd dated in high school to a man. Very definitely a man. Being near him caused a humming inside Alora that she found very disconcerting, especially after the last two years of forced celibacy.

The home itself had surprised her when they arrived; she'd noticed it over the years, a grand old Victorian style with turrets and a gorgeous covered porch. The over grown gardens, and paint peeling off the siding added to the charm of the home. She could see what this house could be.

Inside, the central staircase opened to the second floor and Dillon had obviously spent quite a bit of time working on the entry and stairs. The deep cherry wood gleamed with fresh varnish, the walls had been redone with new drywall and were painted a very traditional hunter green.

Dillon had shown her around and so far his renos had focused on getting the entry, the stairs, the master and second bedroom as well as the kitchen, livable. There were a lot of rooms yet to be done, but this house would be a true showcase when finished.

The kitchen had made Alora clench with jealousy, instead of going old school traditional Dillon had chosen white cabinets which covered the majority of the space, the walls he had gone with a dark chocolate brown that almost looked black. The appliances gleamed, the countertops shone and it looked high end but comfortable.

They had glanced in the main floor rooms that still needed to be done, and Alora could see the sheer size of the project Dillon had taken on. The formal living room, the dining room, a powder room and the family room still needed to be done and that was just on the main floor. She did love home renovations though, finding it relaxing and mind numbing. She could get rid of any stress, and allow her mind to focus on other things which allowed the creative aspects to come free, so in some ways she looked forward to helping out.

Alora sighed and stretched, glancing at the bedside clock which read just after ten. With determination, she forced herself out of the bed and stumbled into the attached bathroom. After brushing her teeth and splashing cold water on her face, Alora quickly brushed her hair and tossed on some comfortable clothes.

Then with a steadying breath she stepped into the hallway. Downstairs she heard noises coming from the kitchen.

"Good morning." Dillon looked up at her, from where he stood by the stove, with a slow grin crinkling his eyes. "You must have gone to bed late."

Alora nodded. "I was in the studio. Planning. It's such a great space."

"That it is." He tilted his head at a stool pulled up to the massive island. "Grab a seat. I've got omelettes almost done. And there's coffee on the counter."

"Dillon, you don't have to cook for me." Alora protested.

"Don't have to, no. Want to, yes. Did it, yes. It gets lonely eating by myself and I hate cooking for one. So have a seat."

"Alright. But I'll do the clean-up." Alora poured herself a cup of coffee and sighed with bliss as she hopped up onto a stool.

"Deal." Dillon grinned over his shoulder at her and Aloras stomach performed a series of gymnastics from how scrumptious he looked. His low slung sweat shorts and tank top showed a body just as good as she'd imagined it to be. Alora found it oddly intimate sitting in the kitchen while Dillon cooked breakfast. His bare feet attested to the fact that he wasn't going anywhere anytime soon.

She slid her eyes towards said bare feet, and found herself oddly comforted. A lot of men had gnarly feet with bunions and growths and an incredibly offensive odor. The distance made it impossible to tell about the smell, but his feet were smooth and appropriately sized. No growths that she could see. Dillons feet looked like him, well kept, smooth and strong without being overwhelming. She didn't have a foot fetish, she had just noticed over the years that you could tell a lot about a man from his feet.

Dillon flipped two omelettes onto plates and turned back to Alora. "All done. Did you need ketchup?"

Alora shook her head as Dillon handed her the plate. "No thanks, they smell great."

Dillon slid onto the stool next to Alora and dug into his food with gusto. Comfortable silence settled over them as they ate.

Finally just about finished Alora sat back with a sigh, her coffee cup in hand. "That was delicious Dillon. Thanks."

"No problem. How did you sleep?" His green eyes stared into Aloras with an intensity that made her clench.

"Good. You?"

"Great. I've got to get some work done, so I'll be closeted in my office for most of the day." Dillon smiled and took his last bite of breakfast.

"What is it that you do?" Aloras curiosity took over.

"I develop software. I have thirty days till my next product launch, so I've got a lot of work to get done. I usually split my day, at my computer until four or five, then I work on something in the house for a few hours before having a late supper."

"Software? Like what types? Keep it English and not too much technospeak so I can understand." Alora smiled at him, glad to know that although he may have changed physically, the geek she fondly remembered still existed on the inside.

"Mostly systems for large corporations. Things that help them run more effectively, or help with staffing issues etc. It depends on what they are looking for, I work for an American company that hires the jobs then farms them out to me." Dillon's voice gathered in an excited manner. "Right now I'm working on software that will prevent viruses in a huge conglomerate. Essentially it routes all unusual IP addresses within certain parameters and tags them for a sweep with the new software. I won't go into technical details, but it is coming along great."

"Wow. I'm glad you're doing what you always wanted to do." Alora's eyes softened as she said. "I remember how much you always loved your computer."

"I did. I was such a dork." Dillon looked at the counter a small frown on his lips.

Alora reached out a hand and touched his arm, sending a shiver through her at the warmth under her fingers. "Not a dork. You knew what you liked and you didn't care what others thought. I always admired that about you."

Dillon stared at her fingers lightly brushing the hair on his arm for a minute until his eyes swung up to meet hers. His normally soft green eyes had darkened to an almost forest green and she pulled her hand away.

"Sorry." She mumbled, embarrassed, and stood up.

Dillon grabbed her arm, and spun her closer, his other hand capturing her cheek, tilting her face up towards his. Her eyes a window to her shock, Alora looked up at Dillon and felt that swift sharp pang of her libido switching into high speed, deep in her loins.

With a sigh he lowered his mouth to hers in a soft soul sucking kiss. Their lips touched and explored, gently becoming reacquainted with one another. Unable to resist, Alora's hands threaded through Dillon's hair, its silky lengths sliding through her fingers. Dillon moaned and wrapped one arm around her waist and pulled her closer.

His hard body scorched her wherever they touched, as Dillon deepened the kiss, tracing the outline of her lips with his tongue. Alora sighed and her lips parted allowing him entry. Another groan sounded, this time from both of them as they kissed. Alora breathed in the scent that was all Dillon, musky with a hint of mint.

All too aware of her forced passionless life, it had been so long since she had felt like a woman. Too long since she had felt the heady rush of desire coursing through her veins and with a whimper she let go surrendering to the passion that swirled through her.

A delicious heat spread out from within her and she plastered her body against Dillon's and twirled her tongue with his. His hard angles fit perfectly against her soft curves, and Alora felt passion spreading.

Finally Alora came to her senses and pulled away. Breathing heavily she leaned her forehead against Dillon.

"What are we doing?" She whispered raggedly.

"Uh. Kissing?" Dillon muttered, his breath short.

"Well. Duh." Alora smiled softly and took a step back, extricating herself from Dillon's arms. "This is really a bad idea."

"Why?" Dillon demanded.

"We're trying to be friends. And we're living under the same roof. It's a bad idea." Alora turned away, unable to look at the passion in his eyes any longer.

She took a couple steps forcing a distance between them caught up in her thoughts and trying to calm her inner harlot. Silence took over for a few minutes as they composed themselves.

From behind Dillon grabbed her arm, causing Alora to jump and spin around fear in her eyes. Dillon dropped his hand in horror.

"Alora?" His soft voice whispered.

"Sorry. I'm just emotional." She shook her head dislodging the fear.

"Why were you afraid there?" Dillon asked.

"You just…well…you shocked me." Alora whispered.

"Don't bullshit me, Alora." Dillon's emotion filled voice caused Alora to flush. "Why were you afraid? Don't you know I would never hurt you?"

"I know you wouldn't." Alora turned away again.

"Did that bastard hurt you?" Dillon ground out.

Alora didn't say anything. She shook her head mutely unable to talk.

Her ex-husband had been a dick in so many ways, not the least of which was his temper and his drinking habits. Sometimes things had happened and Alora usually ended up hurt, emotionally. They had happened and Wendell had always been so apologetic after that Alora had always forgiven him.

She was upset that she had reacted to Dillon in such a way. She had been sure the jumpiness had been banished and that she would be able to behave normally. She wasn't afraid any longer; she had no reason to freak out like a battered wife. Alora refused to let herself be that person any longer.

Dillon moved around her until she was forced to look at him dislodging her train of thought. His hand turned her chin up lightly. "I would never hurt you."

"I know." Alora focused on his bright green eyes.

"Did he hurt you? Your husband? Please talk to me." Dillon's soft voice questioned.

"No. No. You just shocked me, I'm sorry I jumped. Wendell didn't think I was worth very much, he mostly would yell and call me names. I couldn't do anything right." Alora paused lost in thought before she continued.

"That's when he actually noticed I was there. He made me feel like I wasn't adequate. He told me often enough how bad I was at everything." Alora whispered appalled that she couldn't lie to Dillon and now he knew just how weak, unwanted and insipid she had been.

Dillon wrapped his arms around Alora holding her gently. "No one has the right to make another person feel bad about themselves. Your husband was a bastard and a bully."

Alora nodded neither in agreement or dismissal, then visibly gathered herself and whispered. "I've got to go. I'll see you around four to help with the renos."

"Alora, we aren't done here." Dillon said.

"Yes, we are, I have to go." Alora turned and forced herself not to run from the room.

***

Dillon fought down his anger as Alora scooped up her purse and ran out the door. The thought of anyone making Alora feel like she obviously did, made him see red. He wanted to find the limp dicked bastard and beat the shit out of him.

The fear in her eyes had nearly brought him to his knees; Dillon couldn't stand seeing it there. For a moment he'd been terrified that she'd been physically abused, he didn't know if he could handle that. However grateful he felt that she hadn't had to go through that, he understood that the effects of verbal abuse could be just as horrible. He'd met women in his life who had lost all their self-esteem after a short relationship with a verbally abusive man. Frustrated, he cursed out loud and slammed his fist against the counter top.

He knew he couldn't go to the office just yet; his anger left him unable to focus on programming. So he stalked into the future dining room where he had his punching bag set up. The heavy bag was suspended from the ceiling and moved satisfyingly as Dillon punched at the leather surface.

He felt his anger slowly leach out of his system and he let his mind wander as his body took control.

Kissing Alora had been like tasting heaven. Perfect, her soft body pressed against his erection had been enough to make him nearly blow. It may have been ten years, but the attraction still thrummed between them, her lips were just as soft as he remembered, her moans and sighs of pleasure just as torturous.

When he'd first asked Alora to move in, it had been like old days. The connection he felt, that same smile. Every good memory of high school involved Alora. Even if she broke his heart later – that was university guys' problem.

They had met the summer before Dillon started his senior year. He had been such a geek, he hardly looked up from his games most of his high school career. But that summer he had gotten a job, to save money for university.

He had been serving customers at McDonalds when Alora had come in for her first day. Everyone in town, even Dillon, knew of the McIntoshs, with their huge brood of kids and loud mannerisms. But Dillon had never met any of them. He had trained Alora and they had become close while working together. Soon they were hanging out, outside of work and on a warm July night Dillon had first kissed her. He still remembered that first kiss, at AM Park. A sweet night, Alora had been on the swings when Dillon stopped her and with as much fear as he'd ever felt in his entire life, he'd kissed her enticing mouth.

After that and through his last year of high school they had been inseparable. Dillon had still been a total geek, but Alora hadn't seemed to mind. She played video games with him and they watched movies together.

On Christmas Eve night they'd lost their virginities to one another. His Mom had been working an afternoon shift at the factory and Alora and him had gotten together to exchange gifts. As they looked at the twinkling tree, they kissed and took their first steps into adulthood together. He still remembered her blue eyes twinkling in the soft lights as she whispered that she was fine. Afterwards they had run their hands over each other's bodies in awe of the act, and the love they felt.

Alora had been his first everything, his first love, his first kiss, his first lover. Together they had tentatively discovered what made each other feel good and although they had moments of embarrassment and shyness, they had each other. That year together reigned supreme as one of the best of his young life. Alora had deep passions and enjoyed every moment of her life. She'd been shy, but her sense of humour and personality, once she relaxed was that of a fire ball. He had loved her so much.

In June at his graduation ceremony, he had given Alora a promise ring. The plan had been for him to still go to university and she would join him in Toronto the following year when she graduated. Dillon knew then, as much as any eighteen year old knew, that he would spend the rest of his life loving the woman that stood beside him.

The first few weeks of their long distance relationship went well. They had talked all the time, and wrote numerous letters. In October silence had fallen. Alora hadn't answered his letters or been available when he called.

Finally on November 11th the other shoe had fallen, a letter had arrived. To this day Dillon could still recite the letter, he had unintentionally memorized it almost immediately. He could still see Alora's young swirly handwriting.

Dear Dillon,

I'm sorry to write this letter to you. But I have to. I think it's best if we break up. I can't date you anymore. I've realized we don't really have anything in common. My friends have shown me just how mismatched we are. You are a geek and I am not. I don't want to be with such an antisocial misfit any more.

I've met someone else. He's strong and he treats me like I matter. I don't have to play video games to get his attention. I haven't been cheating on you – I just met him. And I knew I couldn't carry on this farce any longer. I don't love you, I don't think I ever did. You were a placeholder until I could find someone better.

I know you're off in university doing your thing and I wish you the best. Please don't be angry, I just need more than a long distance relationship and you deserve someone who really likes the same geeky things as you do. I don't regret anything we did together. Don't bother calling me, my mind won't change. Good luck in your life.

Alora

That letter had torn him apart. For months that's all he'd been able to see or hear in his mind. He nearly flunked out of class his distress had overwhelmed everything in his life at that point. Finally he had come to the conclusion that he could do nothing, but move on. He had started working out and found such a release in the physical activity that he'd eventually shed the image of geek from his body. He would always be a nerd in mind, but in body he appeared to be the jock. He hadn't carried a torch for her, he'd moved on. But being faced with his childhood dream made it hard to not remember how good they had been together. The Alora he had begun to get to know now, this was the Alora he remembered from when they dated; not the bitch who'd written such a heartless letter.

Just for a few minutes today, in the kitchen Dillon had been as happy as he could remember. Lost in bliss, ready to drag her to his bedroom and make sweet love to her. Then she'd pulled away and he had, discomfort aside, understood that he had moved too fast. If he got involved with Alora again he wasn't sure he would survive the fallout.

So he'd had been inclined to agree with her, not that them being together would be mistake but that they needed to think things through. With their heads and not their bodies. She'd jumped and he knew, instinctively that fear had filled her. The knowledge that Alora had suffered through the years didn't make him happy as he might have once suspected.

He aimed a vicious upper cut at the bag and breathing hard he sagged against it. His arms wrapped around the soft leather surface. Feeling better Dillon pushed his emotions aside and tried to figure out how to help Alora.

He strode back into the kitchen and poured a glass of water. As he drank he leaned against the counter his mind gnawing at the problem.

Chapter 5

Alora clomped up the street, frustrated with herself. She had run out of the house like some chicken shit terrified of her own shadow. Away from Dillon, and the things he made her feel. She knew she had to do something about the attraction that swirled between the two of them but she still had no idea how to approach the subject. His physical attraction constantly distracted Alora whenever he happened to be around.

But Wendell had been good looking too, and looks didn't fool her anymore. She knew ugly people lived on the inside of beautiful faces. Dillon however, seemed to be the same great guy inside as he'd always been. The level of comfort she experienced with him felt natural, like they'd never been apart. Alora would have expected some degree of awkwardness when she moved in but it had been very easy. His green eyes haunted her constantly and she knew she wanted him with a passion that shook her.

She forced thoughts of Dillon from her mind, determined to focus on the sculpture and her process to completing the project. Today she needed to get clay delivered and pick up all her supplies for making the structure.

As she walked she tried to calculate her current bank balance against the necessary purchases, mentally tallying and hoping she had enough.

Distracted she didn't hear the car pull up beside her, until it slowed right down and the window unrolled.

"Alora. Hop in; I'll give you a lift." She looked into the face of Wendell Blakey, her ex-husband.

"No thanks. I'll walk." She turned away resolutely not wanting to talk to him.

"Come on, get in. There's no point in walking when I can give you a ride." His smooth voice called out but Alora ignored him and walked on. His black Lincoln pulled over and Alora heard the door slam as Wendell ran up beside her.

"You're being ridiculous. Why won't you talk to me?" Wendell moved as he had always moved, solidly. A former high school football player, he had maintained his traditional good looks through the years. His blonde hair still fell softly to the left in a bone straight part emphasizing his model perfect cheekbones. His jawline was a thing to behold, defined and masculine. Wendell had always been a beautiful man, which explained how he'd managed to sweep her off her feet so easily. He was five years older than Alora, and when he had started paying attention to her while she had been a lowly high school senior she had seen stars. His wooing had been complete, he made her the focus of all his attentions and she had been blinded by the signs that he might not be as great as he seemed.

"I've called you several times." He added as they walked along.

"I know." Alora replied.

"So why aren't you calling me back?" He asked.

"In case you've forgotten, we're divorced." Alora focused on the sidewalk, wishing he would go away.

"But I need to talk to you." Wendell stepped in front of her, blocking her path so she stopped and looked at him.

"Fine. What is it you want to talk about?"

"There. See you can be nice. I heard you lost your apartment, are you living with your parents?" Wendell's brown eyes looked concerned.

"No, I found a place." She crossed her arms over her chest defensively.

"Oh, I thought maybe you might need somewhere to stay." Wendell looked derailed. "Where are you staying?"

"With a friend. Listen I need to go. I have things to do." Alora started to edge around him.

"What friend? Who are you staying with?" He tilted his head, curiosity filling his eyes.

Alora paused, unsure how to answer, in a small town like Kennedy word would get around that she had shacked up with Dillon. She crossed her arms over her chest and decided that Wendell wouldn't be the first to know.

"It doesn't matter Wendell. I'm staying with a friend."

"Can't we talk? We used to have such great conversations. No one listens to me like you do. I got promoted at work, so much has changed. I really just want to talk." Wendell's voice became soft.

"If you want to talk, you should talk to Heather. You remember Heather? The twenty year old you left me for?"

Cass had dubbed her Heather the Whore, but Alora wouldn't refer to Wendell's girlfriend that way. At least not to his face.

"Wait. I made a mistake. Heather and I broke up. And I was hoping you and I could go out." His eyes were sincere as he leaned towards Alora. She caught a whiff of his go to cologne, that heavy musk of Drakkar Noir.

Her eyes flew to his in shock. "Heather broke up with you?"

"I broke up with her." For a moment his brown eyes hardened in anger, and then they softened as he continued. "What we had was good. I miss you Alora. I really want you to come home; you know you can't survive without me. I take care of you. I'm willing to move slowly if that's what you want, but I want us to get back together."

Looking as though a shovel had hit her in the head, Alora stared at her ex-husband unable to believe he thought she'd come back to him. That explained to her mind why he had gotten her evicted, so she'd need him. Her breath shortened and she flatly stated. "No Wendell. I won't go out with you, what we had wasn't good and I am moving on. Now if you'll excuse me." She stepped around him this time and walked away saying. "I have things to do today."

"This isn't over Alora. You need me, I need you and we will get back together." Wendell called out from behind her but Alora kept walking.

Alora stormed all the way downtown unable to believe the nerve of him. Their entire marriage had consisted of her trying to be everything that Wendell had wanted. The perfect little wife, her hair conventional, her behavior conventional, her every thought conventional. And it still hadn't been enough. When he'd he had left her for another woman Alora had realized just how toxic and emotionally abusive Wendell had been.

After eight years of marriage she had been left with so little self-esteem that she had truly believed she couldn't survive without him. The first month after he'd left she spent curled in a fetal position, in a constant state of tears. She had been convinced no man would ever want her again and that she had been lucky to land a guy like Wendell. She tried in vain to get him back, throwing herself at him and begging him for another chance.

The second month Cass and Brant had convinced her she could live again. It took a long time and working with a counselor but she now recognized that Wendell leaving her had probably been one of the best things that he could ever have done. She had found herself. She was no longer ashamed to admit who she had become, and conventional couldn't be used to describe her. She was different and proud of it.

She still had scars, but one by one with determination, grit and some tears she had learned to face them. More than face them, she had learned to overcome them.

She ran through her errands, ordering the clay and wire for the armature and arranging for its delivery, all the while thinking about the person she had been. With a deep breath she walked into her last stop of the day. The public library. She had sworn two years ago that she would learn to be self-sufficient and not ever be totally dependent on any man again. Step one to achieving this goal meant putting herself out there.

A few hours later safely ensconced back in her new studio, her products had been delivered and a she had a list of websites to check out on how to set up an artist page. After some research, reading and talking to other artists online she knew the only way to be taken seriously by the rest of the world would be to start treating herself as a serious artist. She had to stop doubting her abilities and show the world what she could do.

She smiled and set the paperwork aside before picking up her cell phone and hitting speed dial one. She had so far avoided telling her parents she had moved but the time had come. After the third ring her Dad picked up with a brusque. "Hello?"

"Hey Dad, it's Alora. How are you?"

"Good. You?" Alora could hear the television being muted in the background.

"I'm okay. I was just calling to let you know I've moved. I rented a room with … a friend. I have access to a studio to work in."

"Brant and Cass came here all in a dither about you two days ago."

"I figured." Alora snorted. "I'm fine. I just wanted to let you know I'd moved so you and Mom don't worry."

"Why don't we come over there tonight? We can help you get settled in."

Alora shook her head, and then answered. "No thanks Dad. Listen I am renting a room in a house, not the whole house. It seems wrong to have all of you invade when I really only have a bedroom."

"We don't see enough of you, are you sure you're okay? If you need money I can come up with-"

"No." Alora's firm voice allowed no arguments. "I'm fine. I don't need any money. Thank you though. I will see everyone on Sunday for dinner. Will you do me a favor and let the top three and the bottom two know that I've moved? I don't want to freak them out and I need to get going on this sculpture." Alora crossed her fingers that her Dad would take the dreaded calling off her hands which would give her four days of peace from her siblings.

"Sure, kiddo. If you're sure that's all you need…" Her Dad's soft voice assured Alora that he would do anything for her.

"I'm sure, Dad. Thanks. Gotta go. Time to get working on this sculpture. I'll see you Sunday. Give Mom a kiss from me."

"I will. You call me if you need anything. See you Sunday."

Alora hung up the phone, relieved. Her familial duty done she turned to the armature and began cutting and forming the framework that would give her sculpture structure.

Her thoughts kept trying to go to the steamy kiss she had shared with Dillon this morning. Resolutely she pushed the disturbing, but ever so erotic, images from her mind and focused on her work.

***

Dillon stretched, his back making an audible and comforting crack as he looked at the time on his laptop. 4:30, he smiled and saved all the work he'd gotten done then shut down the computer. Today he planned on starting the work on the formal living room. The old lathe and plaster had to be pulled off in preparation for the new drywall.

He stood up and shut the door to his office as he left. All day his thoughts had circled Alora and so far he'd been unable to come up with a solution. He knew in his mind that Alora didn't need saving: and he wouldn't pretend to be a superhero ready to sweep in and save the day. But that didn't prevent him from wanting to help her out.

A delicious smell invaded his brain as he approached the kitchen. He rounded the corner and leaned on the doorway watching as Alora, her back to him, stirred something in the crock pot. She wore a faded pair of blue jeans that fitted perfectly to her round ass and a loose t-shirt that had seen better days.

"Hey." He called from the doorway not wanting to scare her again.

Alora turned and smiled at him, her eyes wary. "Hey. How was your day?"

"Productive. What's in the pot?" Dillon moved closer.

"It's chicken stew. I hope you don't mind, but since you made breakfast I took the initiative and threw together some supper. I used the slow cooker so it would be ready whenever we were done working on whatever project you had in mind for tonight."

"Sounds, and smells, great." Dillon grinned at her. "I had no idea you were so domesticated."

Alora snorted. "Hardly. One dish meals are the extent of my culinary abilities I'm afraid. If it involves too many dishes I'm guaranteed to screw it up, as I've been told way too many times. But I am the Queen of Casseroles."

Dillon ignored the barb on her abilities and said instead. "Thank you, you didn't have to. I appreciate it."

A light pink blush appeared on her cheeks as she looked at the ground. "You're welcome." She looked up at Dillon. "What did you want to work on tonight?"

"I thought maybe some demolition. The front living room, pulling out the old plaster."

"Okay. I'm good at demolition." Alora grinned, then the smile faded from her lips as she took a breath. "Before we go further. I am sorry about this morning. I may have given you the wrong impression. I was not a battered woman or anything like that. So many women had it worse than I did. I will not be labeled. Yes, over our eight year marriage Wendell did hurt me emotionally. He did not beat me. I am a woman who is ready to take control of her own life. I will be strong, and survive."

Alora sighed then continued. "We had our fights, and our marriage didn't survive. I neither want, nor need your pity. Because there is nothing to feel sorry for." She looked away momentarily before her blue eyes met his again, this time with steel in them. "I'm not going to talk about this subject beyond what I am saying now and to say the subject is closed. It is not up for discussion."

"But Alora," Dillon began until Alora glared at him.

"That's it. Discussion done. I will not discuss my marriage or my failures with you, or anyone." Her voice whipped across the room.

"Okay." Dillon held up his hands. "Fine. I won't push the subject. But if you want or need to talk, know that I am here."

Alora nodded then smiled softly. "Okay. Lets' get started. Where's the sledgehammer?"

***

A few hours later they were filthy with dust and laughing. The living room had been stripped down to the bare studs and all the bits of plaster had been put in the bin parked in the driveway. They had worked well together, Dillon found himself quite happy that Alora wasn't the type to shy away from hard work.

They had each jumped into their respective showers for a quick clean up and had met down in the kitchen to eat.

Dillon handed Alora a bowl filled with stew when she came into the kitchen. Her wet hair hung down past her shoulders, her face shiny and refreshed as she grinned at him.

"Do you mind if we eat in the family room?" She asked.

"Thank god, that's what I was hoping for. I normally watch television while I eat supper." Dillon grabbed the bowl and led the way. The family room had yet to be redone, the wallpaper from the eighties attested to that fact. They sat on the couch and Dillon grabbed the remote.

"Nice tattoo." Dillon pointed with the remote towards Alora's bare feet.

"This?" She held her foot out so Dillon could see the inked area better. He admired the scrolling letters on the top of her slim foot, and then he laughed.

"As you wish? That's what you get tattooed on you? Now whose love are you dying for?" She kicked at him.

"No one's but my own. I assume you've watched *The Princess Bride*, then?"

"Of course." Dillon smiled. "Hello, my name is Inigo Montoya..."

"You killed my father, prepare to die!" They completed the quote together, laughing.

"It really is a great movie." Dillon added.

"One of my favorites." Alora sighed. "It taught me about loving myself more than I love anyone else. That I have to come first to someone and that might as well be me."

Dillon cleared his throat before changing the subject. "Is there anything specific you want to watch?" Dillon asked as he flipped on the television to distract himself from the strawberry vanilla scent that wafted from Alora.

"Um." Alora hung her head, hair covering her face shyly.

"Oh, come on. Spill it." Dillon nudged her.

"The new episode of *Doctor Who* is on tonight." She said quietly. "Normally I PVRed it since Wendell couldn't stand the show, but I don't have a PVR, so I was hoping you wouldn't mind..."

"Since when do you watch *Doctor Who*?" Dillon exclaimed.

"Oh please. You know I've accessed my inner geek. You saw me as Catwoman." Alora laughed.

"A sight I'll not soon forget." Dillon felt his loins tighten at the memory. He flipped the channel just in time to catch the opening sequence.

They watched and ate in silence, companionably enjoying the show. Dillon was distracted and missed much of the plot since Alora sat beside him, shifting and sighing and smelling so amazing he had a hard time keeping his hands off her. As the end credits rolled Dillon flipped the TV off and turned towards Alora.

"I haven't told you, but I really do like your hair that colour."

"Thanks. I did it when I became single again. I was tired of being the plain Jane." She tucked a loose strand behind her ear. "I've wanted to do it for years. I love it."

"So do I." Dillon reached out and let a loose strand curl around his finger. "It suits you. But you didn't need to change; you were never as plain as you thought. Alora you always stood out in a crowd."

Alora swallowed audibly and took a breath. "You know maybe we should talk." She whispered.

"Talk?" Dillon longed to touch her, his fingers were on fire from the soft whisper of her hair against his skin.

"Yes. Talk." Alora's breathy voice tickled Dillon's ears.

Dillon took a deep breath, calming his inner beast, and sat back. "Okay what would you like to talk about?"

"Um. Well, we are obviously attracted to each other." Dillon nodded emphatically in agreement, and laid his arm along the back of the couch nearly touching her shoulder as she sat facing him. "So, what are we going to do about it? The attraction I mean. Can we ignore it?"

"I can't." Dillon felt his loins tighten just talking about the physical pull he felt from Alora. "I say we just do it." He grinned, attempting a joke to lighten the mood, but Alora just nodded solemnly then spoke.

"All day I've tried to ignore it and it hasn't worked. You distract me." Her eyes met his briefly before she looked away again. "I can't focus. I think maybe we need to make a deal."

"I'm listening." Dillon's eyes squinted suspiciously.

"Okay. So here's what I think. Maybe we could be friends...roommates with benefits." Shock filled Dillon's eyes, of all the things she could have suggested this didn't even end up on the list. He never would have suspected anything like this had gone through Alora's brain. She continued unaware of the sudden pulse of pure lust from Dillon. The thought of having Alora in his bed again overwhelmed him. "I'm only here for sixty days. We are attracted to each other, right?" Her eyes flashed to his long enough for Dillon to nod mutely before she looked away a pink tint on her cheeks testifying her embarrassment. "We are both adults. Neither of us is in a committed relationship. We are living in the same house, so I recommend a purely physical relationship. No emotions. No promises. Just us, both getting what we want. And at the end of the sixty days, when I move out, we both move on, no regrets. Friends."

Silence filled the room for long moments while Dillon tried to digest her offer. The silence stretched on until finally Alora spoke.

"If you don't want to, don't worry about it." Her voice bubbled over in a fast fashion. "It's okay. You don't have to. I just thought... never mind. It was stupid. Forget I said anything. I am so stupid."

"Alora." Dillon put a finger over her lips to make sure she stopped the verbal diarrhea that poured from her mouth. "First, don't ever say you're stupid. Second, you caught me off guard, I was trying to process."

Alora nodded silently giving him a chance to think over her suggestion. Having her back had at one time been the only thing on Dillon's mind. That was a long time ago, now he found himself being drawn back into her web. Wanting her, wanting to be with her but not wanting to be hurt by her. He thought for long moments while he studied the way she played with a loose thread on her jeans.

Finally he spoke. "Well you've certainly shocked me tonight. And the answer is yes."

Chapter 6

Alora held her breath in shock and pleasure. He said yes. For a few moments there she had thought for sure the next words out of his mouth would be 'thank you, but no.' Her nerves had gotten the better of her and she had started to babble, embarrassed enough that she had hoped the floor would open up and swallow her whole.

After running into Wendell today she had decided she had to move on. She had managed to recover most of her self-esteem, but her insecurities when it came to her sexuality were still paramount. When he had offered to date her again, she knew she had to take the leap and try to be a sexual woman again before she ended up accepting Wendell's offer simply because she didn't think that anyone else who would want her.

All day she had wrestled with the problem, and with her attraction to Dillon, until finally this idea had come upon her. Even now it felt like the air between them hummed with electricity. She could feel him looking at her as she nervously fidgeted with a torn piece on her jeans. Finally she realized the silence had gone on for too long so she met his green eyes and said.

"Okay, great." She tried to smile, it may have come out more like a grimace, her nerves seemed to have gotten the better of her. "So how do we go on from here?"

"Well. I think we need to set up some ground rules and expectations." Alora's stomach clenched. "I'm not sure what you had in mind and I don't want any misconceptions." Dillon looked towards her then took her hand in his big one and slowly ran his thumb over the tender skin on the back of her hand gently. While this calmed her nerves it did nothing for slowing her libido which jumped and pulsed out of control.

"Okay." Alora said quietly. "What did you have in mind?"

"A few things, first I want you to move into my bedroom. I don't want a booty call in the middle of the night before you rush back to your own room." Alora nodded agreeing with the understandable condition. "Your turn."

"Um," Alora mumbled, she hadn't thought about anything besides being able to have a sexual relationship again. "I guess, well, I don't want you to take care of me. I am working on being independent and don't want or need to feel like a child or an appendage or anything other than an equal." She paused. "Your turn."

"That's not a problem." he smiled at her gently. "I want you to unpack. Especially the boxes marked collections. I want to see what you consider collectable."

Alora grinned at this one then snuffled a laugh. "That's not a problem, although you might ask me to repack it all when you see it."

"I doubt that, unless of course it's your collection of Toronto Maple Leaf memorabilia, then maybe." Dillon returned her grin. "Your turn."

She fell silent for a few moments trying to figure out how to word her next idea. Finally she said. "I've never done anything like this before. A friend with benefits thing, I mean. So this request is kinda two fold."

"I'll allow it." Dillon's thumb continued to softly rub back and forth as they talked. She found it distracting and comforting at the same time.

"So if I do anything that doesn't fit in with the terms, something wrong, will you let me know?" She hung her head embarrassed.

"Hey," Dillon waited until Alora looked at him. "There is no right or wrong. There's only us. We do this our way, the way it feels good to both of us or not at all. And there is no need for you to be embarrassed."

"Okay." Alora smiled shyly then dropped her eyes and rushed through the final part of her request before she could chicken out. "The final part of mine is that you be patient with me. I'm not very good at this kind of thing and I have a lot to learn. I've been told I'm not the type of woman who is great in bed. Plain Jane and cold fish has been thrown around a lot. And it's been a long time, and I, well, I'm afraid I'll disappoint you."

"Again, there is only us. There is no right or wrong and you won't disappoint me. You could never disappoint me." Alora sighed with happiness and leaned slightly towards

Dillon. She allowed herself to relax slightly while she felt the heat from his body emanate towards her, warming her and making her long for more.

"I only have one more 'condition' or thing to tell you. I am not the young boy I was when we first met. I am a demanding lover; I only ask that you have an open mind."

"What, like whips and chains kind of open mind?" Alora asked, shock through her voice, she had never experienced anything like that before. The thought of whips and chains did nothing for her, although perhaps some silk ties. That experience had been one she'd always wondered about.

"No." Dillon chuckled, his voice rumbling deep in his chest. "No whips and chains." He paused for a moment then continued. "When we were together, it was a first for both of us, we had barely explored anything beyond missionary. I have expanded my bevvy of Kama sutra tantric type positions."

Alora's eyes widened with shock. "Um, I'm willing to try. I just don't know much about that."

"That's okay, I do. I like sex a lot, and I want a woman who wants to make love as much as I do. A woman who will embrace her sexuality and be willing to let loose."

Alora held her breath; Dillon had just verbalized everything Alora had wanted this experience to be. She whispered. "All I can do is try. I can't promise you I will be perfect, but I can promise to give you everything I have to give."

"Perfect." Dillon smiled at her, his eyes crinkling with the motion. "I'd also like to add that I think we should leave all conditions up for debate at any later time needed. I want us to be open with each other."

"Okay." Alora knew she would try desperately to give all she had to him and to hide her embarrassment.

"So, one final question." Alora looked at Dillon as he spoke, curiosity in her eyes. "Are you on birth control? And I am assuming you are safe?"

Alora felt a blush tint her cheeks. "I'm not on the pill." She didn't add that birth control of any form would be unnecessary, after all this temporary arrangement meant Dillon had no need to know all about her failings. She continued calmly. "I am safe, after I found out Wendell was sleeping around I got myself checked and got a clean bill of health."

"I too have been checked and am fine. I can show you the report from my doctor. I would like to ask that you see your doctor, and start on birth control again."

"Okay, I'll do that as soon as I can get in to see the doc." She paused. "Until then…"

"Until then we can use condoms." Dillon said matter of factly.

"All right. So now what?" Alora looked up at Dillon, apprehensively.

"Now, we seal the deal with a kiss." Dillon leaned towards her. He reached up and cupped her face between his hands. His lips touched hers softly at first, feather light kisses that melted all remaining nervousness from Alora. Slowly he slipped his lips across the corner of her luscious lips and then covered her mouth with his.

Alora felt warmth spread from stomach, an aching need within her. She looped her hands around his neck and opened her mouth slowly reacquainting herself with the mesmerizing taste of Dillon.

For minutes they lost themselves in kissing, their passion building higher as they moved closer together. She leaned in to Dillon's body, pressing as closely as possible. His hard planes molded against her body perfectly.

Dillon's one hand buried in her hair, as she shifted her increasingly warming body. His other hand traced down her arm and back up her side to slowly cup her breast. She pulled her lips away and groaned.

His breath came hard as he rained kisses along her throat, until he licked a path right back to her lips and nibbled on the lower curve. Alora panted and her hands fisted in his hair lightly.

As his fingers trailed lightly across the strip of bare skin just below her shirt causing a tingling sensation, his eyes met hers. His were darkened with passion, without breaking eye contact he took the hem of her shirt and striped it over her head.

Alora dropped her eyes, she had gained some weight since high school and at twenty eight parts of her body weren't where they once were. Worry filled her as she wondered if she could possibly meet up to his expectations. Self-doubt filled her as she moved to cross her arms over her chest.

"I'm sorry." She muttered, looking away. "I don't look-"

"Wait." Dillon interrupted, cupping his hand under her chin and lifting her face until she looked him in the eyes again. "You are so beautiful." He murmured his voice a low growl in his throat.

A slight smile lifted the corner of Alora's mouth. "Thanks." She whispered. "You're not too shabby yourself."

She reached out and deftly removed his t-shirt, revealing well defined muscles that made her heart pound. Dillon obviously worked out regularly. His pectoral muscles jumped under her tentative touches and his stomach muscles contracted as she ran a finger down the center line.

Her lacy black bra shifted against her skin as she panted with lust. Dillon traced a thumb over the taut peak then cupped the fullness in a firm hand. He lowered his mouth and took her aching tip into his mouth. Pulling lightly on the fabric and her nipple underneath with his teeth, Alora thought she would explode into pieces. She moaned his name in ecstasy and her breasts thrust closer to him. He reached behind her and with one hand undid her bra, sliding it down her arms and dropping it on the carpet.

Alora leaned into him, feeling his manliness pressed against the sensitive skin of her chest with a sigh, as she licked his neck. Their lips met again with a need that quickly escalated.

"Upstairs." Dillon pulled his mouth away long enough to pant. "We...upstairs...bed...now."

Alora nodded but didn't stop the assault on his delicious lips. Finally Dillon growled and pulled away completely. He grabbed her hand and hauled her to her feet. Then he leaned down and kissed her again. Alora couldn't get enough of his lips; she threw herself into the kiss, her arms locked around his head as she took in his intoxicating taste and scent.

Dillon urged her closer, his hands sliding down to cup her ass. Alora's eyes flew open in shock, and then closed again in bliss as she leaned closer. She could feel his erection through the sweat pants he wore and it made her nearly weep with want.

His hands ventured lower, cupping and lifting her legs until he wrapped them around his waist. Carrying Alora, without breaking the kiss he walked up the stairs. Alora, lost in the moment barely registered the fact that they were moving. She took his earlobe between her lips and suckled deeply, reveling in the whimpering sound of lust Dillon made. She licked the shell of his ear and took a leisurely tour of the surrounding vicinity before returning to his lips once more.

A door opening brought her out of the sex fiend induced stupor she had been reduced to. She opened her eyes and barely registered that they were in Dillon's bedroom. Her feet hit the floor and Dillon dropped to his knees. He kissed a path between her hip bones, the softness of his lips tickling her sensitive spots. His hands worked on her jeans and they soon hit the floor. She stood there in all her glory as Dillon groaned.

"My god, no panties." He sighed, his breath floating across her bare skin. "That's it. You should never wear panties ever." His hands touched and caressed as his lips ran all over her. "And this," he murmured, "Is incredible." His tongue lapped across the small bright blue butterfly tattoo on her hip.

Alora's head fell back, her eyes closed in bliss as Dillon worshipped her bare skin as though no other woman existed anywhere in the world.

A gentle flit of fingers over the opening of her sex had her head whipping back up. "Dillon." She mouthed his name, her voice higher than normal as her hips thrust wantonly towards his hands.

He smiled up at her and widened her stance so that she found herself bared to him. "I love that you are bare down here." He ran his palm over her pelvis.

"Me too." Alora whispered her voice low as she panted. She watched as he drew a finger across her lips. Back and forth, he drove her crazy as she pushed her body closer to his questing digits.

He leaned closer and breathed on her over heated sex. "Oh my." Alora moaned as he buried his tongue inside. He flicked her clit with the tip of his tongue and Alora squealed, her legs trembling.

Dillon pulled his head back and looked up at Alora. "Don't move." He commanded.

She fought the overwhelming urge to grasp his hair and force his questing tongue closer, faster. But Dillon ignored her pleading whimpers and slowly traced the lines of her sex. He suckled on her lips, pulling and tugging gently with his lips and gently nips from his teeth. His tongue plunged inside her and he hummed softly causing Alora to swear as her legs gave out.

Dillon's hands held her up as he moved, and his tongue licked a path from the opening of her sex to the sensitive nub at the apex of her thighs. He licked and suckled until Alora couldn't have formed words if the world ended. Just as her body tightened and her hips flexed, he slid a finger inside her, and whispered, "Now Alora, come for me."

As though his words gave her permission, her body released, seeming to shatter into a thousand pieces, the lights dimmed and she grabbed his head and held it close to her, yelling loudly as she came.

After her body stopped pulsing she looked down at Dillon whose head rested on her thigh with a grin on his lips. "Wow." She shifted her head. "When did I get on the bed?"

Dillon just grinned and stood up. A ripping sound echoed through the room as he dropped his sweat pants and rolled a condom on his long and ever so ready penis.

He looked at Alora, "I hope you're ready."

Then he crawled across the bed towards her, his body shaking with barely suppressed need. He looked at her and she smiled her ascent her arms opening to welcome him.

"You are the most beautiful woman I have ever seen." He murmured as he positioned himself between her knees. "You taste like heaven. It turns me on so much."

Alora could feel herself getting wet again with want as he talked to her, his fingers touched lightly on her desire hardened nipples before running down her bare thighs. He grabbed her ankles lightly and placed them on his shoulders. Then without warning, he plunged deep inside her welcoming warmth.

Alora moaned at the fullness, the perfection of being fitted with a man like Dillon. It had been so long since she had felt this sense of rightness. So long since she'd felt the power and closeness that came from being sexually active. She couldn't look away from him; his eyes burned her with pure need. His body unlike any that she had seen before. She knew him and yet found it to be a completely new experience.

He withdrew, held still for a moment, his penis flirting with the edge, his eyes never leaving hers, and then plunged again. She whimpered, wanting him to thrust faster. But he held his pattern. Thrust, retreat, repeat. Thrust, retreat, repeat. He set a tortuous pace that soon had Alora begging, her fingernails digging into his arms as she tried to force her release.

"Please Dillon. I'm so close." She cried, she could feel her internal muscles clamping down on his manhood in an attempt to hold him closer.

He groaned and plunged inside her, his pace finally meeting her frantic need. He thrust again and again, faster and harder, burying himself as deeply as possible inside her warm wetness. His hands tightening on her ankles until it almost hurt, his body pure perfection outlined in sweat and glowing in the faint light. Finally she felt her muscles tighten again and together they fell over the edge, into a mind numbing orgasm. Dillon roared his release and collapsed on top of her holding her close as his body pulsed deep within her emptying his seed.

For long moments they stayed entangled catching their breath. Until Dillon gave her a quick kiss on the lips and withdrew. He stood and walked into the ensuite bathroom, where Alora could hear water running as he cleaned up.

She lay there, a pile of boneless jelly, unable to believe how much she had missed sex. It had been two long years. She had no idea how she had managed to convince herself that her toys were just as good as having an actual man inside her. She knew now there had never been a contest and she had only been fooling herself. Dillon was an amazing lover; he held her off just long enough and teased a mind blowing orgasm out of her not once, but twice.

When they had been kids together discovering the act of love things had been very different. Back then it had been pure missionary and quick trysts, hoping no one caught them. She thrilled at the differences she noticed. Dillon had grown into the man that had been promised when they were young, confident and experienced and so decadently good.

The bed depressed behind her and Dillon gathered her into his arms. With a contented sigh Alora snuggled closer.

"Are you all right?" Dillon asked softly.

"Mmm hmm." Alora mumbled with a soft smile.

"Did you want to talk?" His breath against her ear both distracted and comforted at the same time.

Alora shook her head lightly. "No talk. Sleep." She muttered sleepily. "Wore me out."

Dillon chuckled then kissed her ear and pulled her closer as she drifted off to sleep.

Chapter 7

Dillon smiled as he walked up the street. If he had the ability he would be whistling a happy tune. It had been three days of bliss since Alora had propositioned him. Three days of amazing sex, companionship and laughter. They had discovered they had a great many mutual interests. Her work ethic matched his own; they had worked tirelessly and gotten the drywall up in the living room.

When she had finally unpacked her boxes of 'collectables' he had nearly died with laughter at the Doctor Who memorabilia, then when she started to get defensive he had taken her to the media room. Well, in most houses it would be a media room, in Dillon's house the room had become a showcase for his vintage Star Wars items and huge comic collection.

He rounded the corner, lost in thought, but still smiling. In bed Alora still held back, being a naturally reserved person, she waited while Dillon took the lead. She didn't seem to have any confidence in herself, which astounded Dillon. Her warmth, receptivity and adventurous spirit made her everything he'd ever wanted in a partner. This was the problem. He wanted to date her, officially. Not be a friend with benefits. He wanted all of Alora, not just the sex. The emotions, the promises, the baggage, he wanted it all. At the end of the sixty days he didn't want Alora to go back to just being a friend. But he had given his word that he would go along with what she wanted.

As he entered The Slide Sports Bar, he ignored the sound of muted music and pulled up a stool at the gleaming oak and metal bar while he wrestled with the problem.

A twenty something girl, her shiny black hair up in a high pony tail, wearing the referee shirt that marked the bartenders at The Slide, smiled at him as she approached.

"What can I get for ya' honey?" Her eyes slid over Dillon's face and perked up perceptibly.

"Can I get a pint of Moose Head?" Dillon asked with a distant smile, before he looked away. The universal language of the 'not interested' worked well today and the girl shrugged good naturedly.

"Sure thing."

Dillon had finished up work midafternoon and with Alora still engrossed in the carriage house he had ventured out. She had yet to let him see any of her work, claiming it wasn't ready to be seen. So rather than mope around waiting for her, he'd decided to come get a beer and think.

"Dillon Edwards. Just the man we were hoping to find."

Dillon looked up and shuddered internally. Standing beside him happened to be none other than Brant, Alora's twin brother, Cass, her younger sister and Eric, the baby brother. He forced a smile and turned on the bar stool.

"Brant. Cass." He nodded at each of them. "And is that Eric? You certainly grew up." He held out a hand.

Eric stood at least six foot two, topping Dillon's admirable height of six one. His red hair was still as bright as a flame, but he had filled out from the spindly nine year old that Dillon had known.

Brant had also changed. He had always been a jock through school but now he had bulked up with pure muscles. Although shorter than either Eric or Dillon he held himself in a way that let everyone know he wouldn't stand to be fooled with.

Cass stood between her brothers, not seeming to notice they topped her by a good eight or nine inches. Her auburn hair had been cut in a short pixie style that showed off a pretty face currently sporting a snarl.

Eric looked at his hand, and then ignored it. "We need to talk to you."

This didn't bode well. Dillon stood, "There's a booth free. Do you want to sit down?"

The three Mcintoshs swiftly crossed the mostly empty bar towards the available booth with Dillon trailing behind in concern and confusion. All three crowded into one side of the booth and faced Dillon as he sat down. Feeling like he faced the firing squad Dillon squared his shoulders and faced the Mcintoshs sitting opposite him.

"We hear," Brant started, "that you're living with our sister." Three pairs of eyes stared at Dillon fiercely.

"Um." Dillon tried to think of what to say.

"It's all over town." Cass snapped, interrupting him.

"So don't bother denying it." Eric's voice whipped across the table. "Her art supplies were delivered to your house. We know. You can't lie your way out of this."

"I wasn't going to." Dillon held up his hands defensively. "But it isn't what you might be thinking. She moved in - as a roommate. She needed somewhere to stay and I had the space, so I offered her a room." Dillon mentally crossed his fingers; nothing he said could be traced as a lie. It just didn't happen to be the *current* truth.

He tried to look nonchalant as he took a drink of his beer and met each pair of eyes in turn.

"So you two aren't dating?" Brant snapped.

"No, we are not dating." Dillon answered steadily, also the truth.

Cass leaned across the table. "Alora is fragile right now. She hasn't recovered from her assbadger of an ex-husband."

"You hurt her," Brant also leaned forward. "And we'll hurt you back."

"Count on it." Eric cracked his knuckles in an extremely effective attempt at ferocity.

"Listen, guys, and Cass." Dillon nodded at all three. "I have no intention of hurting your sister. I am trying to be her friend."

"So you're not sleeping together?" Brant asked, his eyes glittering.

"Your sister is a grown woman. Why aren't you asking her about her sex life?" Dillon tried to deflect the situation; he truly didn't want to outright lie to them.

"She's refusing to answer our calls." Cass answered. "She's freezing us out."

"She's working real hard on the new sculpture." Dillon toyed with his glass absently. "At my place she has her own studio. She spends most of her time in there."

"We," Cass motioned to her angry looking brothers with a ferocious grin, "are here to make sure you don't hurt Alora. She's been through enough without some nobjockey, that's you by the way, trying to avenge some misplaced sense of manhood that she may have hurt. And we're also here to let you know that we are perfectly capable of burning your balls off with a blowtorch should you choose to hurt her." All three guys cringed at her description.

Brant smiled and said. "As long as your intentions are pure we won't have to hurt you. I am a fireman – I know how to make a body indistinguishable – they'll never know who you were."

"And I," Eric took up the stream of conversation. "I am the worst of the Mcintoshs. You won't have to worry about anyone identifying the body cuz they'll never find it."

Cass grinned, a terrifying mockery of a smile, filled with malice and threats. "Do you remember Daxia?" Dillon nodded; Daxia was the fifth Mcintosh sibling. "She asked me to let you know that she is training to become a veterinarian. And that she has access to and knowledge on how to use surgical tools." She paused dramatically. "You hurt one of us, you hurt all of us. Don't think we aren't watching."

"Now wait a second here." Dillon interrupted. "First off, I told you we are friends. Secondly Alora is not some fragile flower that needs to be protected by the three of you and Daxia. I don't appreciate idle threats."

"Oh, they aren't idle." Brant shook his head lightly without breaking eye contact.

"Fine, real threats then. If you'll recall Alora was the one to hurt me in the past – not the other way around. I am doing everything I can to help her out. Which I don't have to do, and you three come in here like a troop of shitsticks and threaten me. Really?"

Dillon took a deep breath, forcing himself to calm down. "I am sure Alora appreciates your protectiveness. But until she tells me to stay away, I'm there. I get that she's been hurt and so have I. However I have no intention of hurting her further. She's great, funny and I like her. I like spending time with her – as a friend. She and I are both adults and if something should come of our friendship you," he waved a hand at them, "can't stop us. So maybe you should just butt the hell out."

"Butt out?" Cass stuttered, lunging across the table towards Dillon. "Who the hell do you think-"

"He's right." Brant interrupted, putting a restraining hand on Cass's arm. "It is none of our business who Alora lives, dates or sleeps with. We, however are just letting you know the possible consequences of those actions. If you hurt her, you know what to expect. Until then, we are good with you."

Cass took a breath and nodded with her brothers at Dillon.

"Okay then." Dillon held his breath hoping this ended the inquisition.

"So now that that is over with," Brant waved the waitress over. "I could use a beer."

***

The house overflowed with people and voices. All seven Mcintoshs were crowded into the average sized living room. Alora looked around, loving her family but wishing sometimes there was less of them as she sat cross legged on the floor (the only available space) leaning against the corner of the couch. The loud voices rolled over her, not one conversation standing out over the other. The television flashed in the background; luckily it had been muted with the game playing so the boys could watch the score.

Alora had deliberately arrived late so that everyone would be involved in each other and wouldn't focus on her for too long. An unrealistic hope but a hope nonetheless.

Growing up in the Mcintosh family had been an exercise in patience. Five kids meant loud dinners, rambunctious laughs and a lot of shared love. As well as fights, lots of fights and violence had predominated their childhoods. As they grew older the fights had dwindled off, but the loudness had not.

Fatina, the matriarch, had been born out of her time; she should have been born in a time when hippies were in style. Never out of flowing dresses or patchwork jeans and tie dyed prints. She had taught the kids about gardening and taking care of mother earth. Giles, their dad, had always worked in a factory; he had taught them how to change the oil and tires on their cars and about being strong and loyal.

Together their parents had always looked like an unlikely pair, what with Giles fair skin, once bright red hair and serious brown eyes and Fatina's flowing soft brown hair and sun darkened skin. But together they fit and they shared a love with each other that caused envy in all that were lucky enough to see it.

"Are you ready for university?" Cass' voice cut through the din as she directed her question at Eric.

"All packed. And ready." Eric smiled gently, his quiet clear baritone voice cutting through the room.

"You leave tomorrow morning?" Brant looked over.

"Yep." Eric sighed.

"What's with the starting this early? I thought school started in September, at least it did in my day." Brant laughed.

"There are a few intro courses that if I do now I can get them over and done with and come September focus on my actual program." Eric explained. "I'm only taking a partial load for the winter and summer semesters which will allow me to find a part time job and get some of the tedious stuff out of the way."

"That's pretty cool." Cass spoke up. "Sounds like you've thought it all through."

Eric nodded. "I have, although it'll be weird not living at home." Eric winked at their mom. "Not having someone to do my laundry."

"It will be odd." Fatina grinned, her eyes twinkling. "The last of my kids is leaving me to go off to school. Now your Dad and I can have all the wild monkey sex we've dreamed of, when and where we want."

"AH Mom!" All five kids groaned. "TMI." Brant made vomiting noises.

"I'm just kidding." She chuckled. "Honestly it will be strange not having kids around to pick up after and worry about."

"Who are you kidding?" Giles, their Dad muttered. "You'll still worry about them, whether they live at home or not."

"True." Fatina smiled unapologetically.

They all broke into individual conversations for a few moments which Alora let slide over her; a comforting reminder of her childhood. After a bit her Mom called out loudly.

"Brant, when are you bringing home a nice girl?" Fatina asked. Her light brown eyes drilled into Brant from her spot on the couch sandwiched between Daxia and Brant. "I heard you went out with Tracy Lofton. She's seems nice. Or if you don't like her, my branch manager has a niece that she would be happy to set you up with. I think her name was Tilly."

"Enough Mom." Brant groaned and rolled his eyes. His strong, intense voice fit Brant perfectly. "I'm not ready to settle down." Alora was incredibly grateful not to have to deal with set ups from her family at this point. They all felt she should recover from her failed marriage and would date when ready, no one pushed.

"You're twenty eight." Giles pointed out from his recliner in the corner. "By the time your mother and I were your age we had three kids. You definitely aren't too young."

"That was you. I am very much so enjoying my youth. There are just too many beautiful women out there to pick one." Brant grinned then turned to Cass. "Maybe you should tell them about your latest date?"

Cass who sat beside Eric on the small love seat threw a decorative pillow across the room at Brant, who caught it easily with a grin. "There's nothing to tell."

"Oh come on!" Alora called out.

"Dish the details, Cass!" Daxia laughed, a melodic sound.

"Enough." Cass held up her hand. "The guy is a real douche canoe. Our first date went mad awesome, the guy is hot enough to melt butter and he was great to talk to, so I agreed to a second date. The second date bombed so bad, he wouldn't look at me, and spent most of the night texting someone else. It was total bullshit."

Alora smiled, Cass always had the most creative way of speaking. Her insults were inventive to say the least.

"Who was it?" Eric asked. Typically the quiet and reserved sibling he rarely voiced much of an opinion when the whole family was together so when he spoke they all took note. While still young, Eric had a way about him that demanded attention even when he said so little.

"You wouldn't know him." Uncharacteristically Cass blushed and lowered her eyes.

"So what's the harm in giving his name then?" Alora asked.

"What are you hiding?" Daxia laughed.

"Nothing!" Cass defended herself. "He's not from Kennedy." Everyone waited looking at her. "Fine, his name is Ethan Washburn, and he is a shitstick so you may as well stop asking me anything. I won't be seeing him again."

"Methinks thou doth protest too much." Daxia's pale blue eyes twinkled.

"Shut your pie hole." Cass muttered while everyone laughed.

"Seriously." Fatina fanned herself lightly. "I am nearing forty eight. I had five children. And still not one grandchild." Brant and Cass looked sideways at Alora who just looked at the floor unwilling to get upset over ancient history. At least not here in front of her whole family.

"It's time you lot," Fatina shook her finger at all her children, "Got moving. Especially the top three – you're all of an age to marry and bring me grandbabies. Bottom two," She nodded at Daxia and Eric, "You're still too young. So you just take your time."

"Fatina darling." Giles interrupted. "The kids will do things in their own time. The more you bug them the less likely they are to get a move on it. We'd rather they were happy than rush." The whole family deliberately did not look at Alora but she knew they were all thinking about her failed marriage to Wendell.

"True." Fatina smiled.

During a momentary lull, all eyes turned to Alora. Her heart clutched in dismay, the moment had arrived where the whole family drilled her on her life and exploits. She knew she wouldn't, couldn't tell them about her agreement with Dillon. It was none of their business.

Alora felt her libido ramp up just thinking about Dillon. The last four days had been glorious. He'd been patient, and kind, and demanding all wrapped up in the package that epitomized Dillon. They had had crazy intense sex unlike anything Alora had experienced before and she felt a dampness between her thighs just thinking about it. It hadn't been all sex and raunchy bedroom time either, they'd talked, laughed, played video games, read and watched tv. The level of comfort she experienced while being around him reassured her, she felt safe and that she could be herself with him.

She had invited Dillon to come tonight, the family always seemed to have strays joining them for meals, but he had vehemently declined. Saying he had work to do and would see her when she got home.

"So." Daxia tugged on the long ponytail encasing her light brown hair impatiently. "Are you going to tell us?" She looked directly at Alora pulling her out of her thoughts.

"Tell you what?" Alora tilted her head questioningly.

"About the dishy new roommate of yours?"

"There's nothing to tell." Alora hedged. "I moved in, which all of you knew. Dillon is my roommate. That's it."

"Yeah right." Cass slurred her words with innuendo.

"I was in a bind. Dillon has a huge house with space for me to work and is willing to wait until I finish the sculpture to get his rent money. So I moved in." Alora picked absently at the carpet, determined not to remember the image of Dillon naked while in the room with her family.

"This is the same Dillon you were so hot for in high school?" Giles asked.

"Yes, we dated. But that was a long time ago." Alora turned to her dad and firmly pushed any naughty images from her brain. "We are adults now."

"And Mr. Dillon is certainly nothing to frown at in the looks department." Cass muttered. "He certainly hunked up since high school." She waggled her dainty eyebrows lasciviously.

"How would you know?" Alora frowned.

"Um." Cass looked at her brothers in a silent plea for help that made Alora's hair stand on end.

"We ran into him at The Slide." Brant shrugged his shoulders nonchalantly. "Yesterday. We had a chat."

"Oh. My. God." Alora shook her head. "What did you say to him?"

"We just warned him."

"We chatted and had a beer with him."

"We questioned him."

Three voices, Brant Eric and Cass overlapped each other's as they tried to explain at the same time. Daxia guffawed loudly until Alora glared her into silence.

"So you questioned him about his intentions, then you threatened him, and then had a beer with him." Alora stated. "Listen guys, thanks, but I am an adult. I can take care of myself. I don't need you meddling. Besides, I am there to work." Alora's voice whipped across the room with such ferocity that her family looking at her in shock. "If I chose to have a relationship with anyone it isn't your concern. It's my choice. Not that I am in a relationship with Dillon. But if I was there would be nothing you could say about it."

"Now Alora, don't get your panties in a bunch." Brant held out his hand calmingly, "We were just trying to look out for you. We don't want you to get hurt again."

"Next time, instead of interrogating my roommate maybe you could ask me."

"Sure we could," Cass snapped back, "if you'd answer your damn phone. Or return messages."

Alora looked away guiltily. "Sorry. I should have called you back. I am trying to get to work now that I have the space. I've been swamped. But that doesn't excuse you from butting into my personal life. You could have pissed off my landlord and gotten me evicted. Is that what you wanted?" All three looked at Alora with guilt written clearly on their faces as they mouthed sorry.

"Okay kids." Fatina stood up. "Kiss and make up, the lot of you. No more fighting on Eric's last night in town."

Alora smiled softly at her siblings and they grinned back so they all knew all had been forgiven. It had always been this way with the lot of them, they picked at each other but they honestly cared about one another. They were family.

"You're all a bunch of meddling old ladies." She laughed at the outrage that flashed across Brant's face.

"And you dear twin are nothing but a self-righteous ball buster."

"Lickspittle arserag." Cass laughed.

"Nice!" Eric exclaimed and high fived Cass.

"Moose faced whore." Daxia's melodic voice sounded.

"Just shut up, the lot of you dickwads." Alora threw back at them with a laugh.

"Lame." Brant grinned. "No points for that pitiful excuse for an insult!"

"All right, kids." Giles interrupted tilting his reading glasses down on his nose. "You suck at the insult game. Always have, none of you can top me. You are all nothing but a bunch of ditch diddlers."

Everyone groaned. "Boo!" Voices shouted out from all the different sides of the room.

As usual Fatina ignored the barbs her kids threw around with ease. Her flowing hippie skirt skimmed the floor as she moved through the room. "Supper should be just about ready. Eric and Brant you set the table. Alora, Daxia and Cass can help dish up the food."

Chapter 8

Dillon paced his physically fit body unable to sit still for long.

"Okay fine, my Dwarf will attack the Paladin, with an axe." He finally declared turning to the group sitting in his living room.

"Dammit Dill. Why are you doing that?" Tyler whined, rolling his twenty sided dice, while the others laughed. "My Paladin just got injured fighting the band of trolls and hasn't had time to get a healing spell."

"I know." Dillon tapped his finger on his chin thoughtfully. "That's why I'm doing it."

"I got a sixteen." Tyler grinned, and then fussed through the character sheet in front of him. "With my bonuses that makes my total a nineteen. Beat that you smarmy Dwarf."

Dillon grabbed his dice and rolled. The die rolled on the coffee table where everyone could see and finally came to a tilting stop on a natural twenty. He whooped while Tyler hung his head and groaned knowing his defeat couldn't be avoided.

When Dillon had first moved back to Kennedy he'd hooked up with his high school friends and joined their regular gaming group. This round they were playing Dungeons and Dragons with Tyler, as their resident Paladin, who had changed from a scrawny long haired Goth kid to a man whose buzz cut and laughing brown eyes seemed in complete opposition to the dark semi suicidal style of his past years. Randy, the game master who had in real life had found Dillon his house, was a tall black haired man with barrel shoulders and a solid build that matched his personality. Joe a blue eyed blonde, whose hair was long but pulled back in a tidy ponytail, owned the local comic book shop, today played a Rogue.

Finally, in complete opposition to most of their high school games, Randy's wife Laura joined them. A robust girl who sported a serious look when it came to gaming. Her short black hair and blue eyes piercing anyone who dared attack her Cleric.

Randy, the game master for this session checked over his numbers. "Paladin is down."

Laura turned to Randy and winked quickly. "I'll heal him." She rolled the dice as she told Tyler. "You owe me."

"Dwarf." Joe barked catching Dillons attention. "Take it down a notch. We're supposed to be a team."

"Dear Cleric, heal me and your every wish is my command." Tyler half bowed from his seat before continuing. "Who invited this guy?" He glared in jest at Dillon.

"Um. Pretty sure this is my house." Dillon laughed to which Tyler just grumbled.

While they calculated out the Paladins remaining health Dillon sidestepped to the kitchen. "Anyone want anything?" He called out to which a chorus of no's echoed back.

As he reached into the fridge the back door opened and Alora came in with a gust of wind. Today she wore a dark blue pair of skinny jeans that molded to her curves like a second skin, emphasizing her soft curves and a Bazinga t-shirt covered in splotches of clay. Her braided hair flipped over her shoulder the bright blue tips catching his eye. She smiled at him and he grinned back.

"Hey." She shut the door.

"Hey, Kitty." Dillon lazed easily against the counter a can of Pepsi in his hand. "How's it going out there?" He nodded towards the studio.

"Step by step." Alora sighed. "Sometimes it all comes so clear, so easily. Other times it's like pulling teeth."

"And let me guess this is one of the latter times." Dillon smiled and crooked a finger beckoning her closer. She nodded as she moved across the kitchen frustration evident both in her face and in the dejected slump of her shoulders.

When she finally got over to Dillon, he set the soda pop behind him to tug her into his arms. Alora sighed and rested her head on his chest with an ease that made Dillon's breath hitch. He slowly stroked her back trying to offer comfort, as her curvaceous body pressed against his; he felt an inevitable reaction to her. A slow, steady and persistent erection pressed between them and he had a moment to feel embarrassed until she looked up at him, her stunning blue eyes clear, and she grinned.

"At least I know, no matter how messy I look or how blocked I feel somebody seems to want me."

"Always." Dillon murmured his voice catching in his throat as he lowered his head unable to resist the lure of her perfect lips any longer. His hand slid up her back to cup the back of her neck and angled her face perfectly before he brought his lips to meet hers. The soft submissive way she gave into the kiss nearly undid him. Her back arched so that her pelvis achieved direct contact with his thigh and she leaned in, her hands braced against his chest. Their lips slid across each other's in a tangle of emotions. His left hand wrapped around her braid and tugged her closer.

"Mmm hmm." Alora sighed against his lips as he snaked his tongue out to trace the lines of her plump lips lightly. She made another needy noise deep in her throat as he deepened the kiss his tongue swirling with hers and her hands fisted in his shirt.

Dillon felt like he had drowned, overwhelmed by the pure heat that Alora caused within him. Her smell enveloped him and he breathed deeply, vanilla and cinnamon. The scent that defined Alora, a little bit sweet and a lot spicy.

"Um. Wow. Excuse me." A voice sounded from behind Alora. "Sorry didn't mean to intrude."

Reluctantly Dillon pulled away and met Alora's eyes still cloudy with unrealized passion. "Later." He mouthed.

He turned and met the laughing gaze of Joe. "Joe, this is Alora, my roommate."

Alora moved towards his friend and held out her hand. "Joe. You own The Heroes Den, right?"

"Of course Alora, the Whovian. Glad to know you recognize me outside of the gloom and dust in the comic shop." He smiled slyly. "I didn't realize you and Dillon were an item." He turned accusing eyes at Dillon.

"She moved in last week." Dillon moved towards her, tempted to put his arm around her, but leaving his arms at his sides instead.

"We're roommates." Alora said softly while Dillon glared at Joe warning him silently to keep his eyes, his hands, his tentacles, his everything off of her.

"Well." Joes eyes twinkled at Alora. "Dillon, you're hoarding the hottest girl around all to yourself? Really man?" He shook his head, jokingly. "Just kidding. Alora, why don't you come in to meet the rest of our motley gang?" He motioned her in front of him and gave Dillon a silent thumbs-up before following her.

"Smooth." Dillon muttered grumpily under his breath as they walked into the family room and introduced Alora around.

The crew managed to convince Alora to play with them, and she created a bow wielding elf, reminiscent of those in the *Lord of the Rings*. She played with abandon, not hiding behind embarrassment as many new players did. Alora threw herself into the game. Dillon found it incredibly hot to see her laughing eyes watch and participate in the game with evident enjoyment.

For five long hours Dillon had been forced to watch her, to see her engaging with his friends and not been able to touch her, or stake any claim to her since they were just friends with benefits.

Dillon had studiously avoided the smirks and sideways glances from his group of friends all day, and finally felt escape nearing as they packed up their supplies and headed out the door.

"I like your friends." Her quiet voice came from behind him as he cleaned up the empty pop cans and bags of chips.

"They are a great bunch." He agreed. "So what did you think of your first DND session?"

Alora tilted her head. "I always wanted to play in school. But, well, I was too busy trying to fit in to admit it." She looked across the room at him, sadness fluttered across her face that Dillon wanted to kiss away. "I'm glad I got the chance now. It was a lot of fun."

She leaned over to pick up Randy's abandoned pizza box until Dillon stopped her with a shake of his head. "I've got the cleanup. While my friends may be cool gaming geeks, they are a tad slobbish." He barked a laugh. "That's why we take turns going to each other's houses, so one person isn't always cleaning up after the rest."

"I can help." Alora asserted, but Dillon shook his head, just as the doorbell rang.

"Ha ha, the bell grants me my choice. You get the door and I'll finish up here." He nodded towards the door.

Alora smirked at him with a shaking head. "Stubborn assed man." But she walked through the house to the front door.

Dillon grinned as she left the room. Living with Alora had been deceptively easy. They got along so well, they fit together. Dillon found himself looking forward to sitting down with her at the end of the night talking about their days. Watching television, cooking, everything they did together seemed as though they'd always done it. He still experienced a thrill thinking about when just two days ago she had given him the all clear to ditch the condoms. She was safe, her doctors appointment must have gone well and he couldn't be happier. Nothing could be better than the feel of Alora without a layer of latex separating them.

After two weeks Dillon found himself convinced more than ever that he wanted more than a pure sexual relationship with Alora. He knew they belonged together and he had to figure out a way to convince her. His fear of pushing her for more than she was able, or willing, to give, that he would lose her altogether left him short of breath. He no longer cared about the girl she had been and why she had broken up with him. All he cared about was the present, the woman she had become. He knew they still needed to talk about their past, if only to get it out of the way, so they would be able to move beyond it. Her letter no longer tortured him, taunting his brain in ways that he couldn't express. He knew they were the words of a girl, not the woman with him now.

Last night, as they lay entwined, after yet another round of mind blowing sex, he had decided to let Alora discover that they were meant to be more than just friends with benefits on her own. To come to her own decision about being in a relationship with him. For now he would play it cool, keep on her terms. He still had a month and a half to show her that they should be more than roommates.

Dillon grabbed the final scrap of paper and tossed it into the recycle bin. Cleanup done, he moved towards the front door wondering what kept Alora.

From the hallway he could see Alora's back as she leaned against the partially opened door. Her stiff body posture as she used her diminutive size to block the entry into the house put him on alarm.

Without thinking Dillon moved closer, wondering who had her on such edge that she stood stiffly.

"Dammit Alora. Let me in." A deep male voice came from the other side of the door way.

Alora shook her head. "No Wendell. Now is not a good time."

"Fine, I'll tell you what I want from outside. Like a simple salesman rather than your husband."

"Ex-husband, Wendell."

He ignored her and continued. "Just last week we talked and we were going to get back together." The voice sounded angry. "And now I find out your shacked up with some twit like a penny whore. I told you then and I'll tell you now, you need me to help you make these decisions. I forgive you for making such unthinkable choices; we both know you aren't smart enough to think things through." Alora hung her head as her ex-husband continued to berate her.

Dillon's blood began to boil; he felt heat slam across his face. *How dare that asshole speak to Alora that way?* He forced himself to calm down; he didn't want to interfere where he didn't belong. He relaxed his fists so they were no longer clenched, and vowed to stand back, to just be support if things got out of hand.

Without hearing Dillon's inner thoughts, Wendell kept on his tirade, with Alora shrinking back. Her shoulders stooped and her head dropped even lower.

"I offered to take you back. To give you the life you deserve. But no, you're too stupid to realize what a favor I am doing you. This guy may want you now, but it's only because you're an easy lay. Soon enough he'll get bored of your cold fish ways and kick your sorry ass to the curb. You may as well stop your rebellion against me now. I am the best that you'll ever get. The only one who'll want you long term. You aren't smart enough or attractive enough to garner long lasting lust."

"Stop it Wendell." Alora finally spoke, raising her head slightly. "You have no right to say these things to me. You left me, remember? I don't have to take you back. I never said I would take you back. Whatever I have, or do, with Dillon is none of your business."

"Dillon?" His voice sneered. "As in Dillon, the nerd, that you were dating when we met? That is the most pathetic thing I have ever heard. You start up with the same geek you used to date, who probably hasn't got laid since high school?"

"You know nothing about him or me or what we have or are doing. You leave Dillon out of this." Alora snapped, some of her spirit showing.

"I don't know anything? I know you sure dropped him quickly enough when I gave you some attention. Hell, he's more than likely sleeping with you now as a revenge thing. Dillon is probably laughing behind your back about how absolutely shitty you are in bed. God knows I tried to teach you. But I know how you work. No one knows you better than me. You need someone with a firm hand to lead you around. To put you on display. To give you everything that they have. You can't make it on your own. I know that you got evicted from your apartment because you can't make enough money in the real world to survive without me. Face it, without me you are nothing."

"Enough. I don't have to listen to this." Alora stood taller. "You don't know me at all. You don't know Dillon. And you have no say in my life. I would like you to leave."

"I'll leave when I'm good and damned ready to, and not a minute before, you fat little slut. You remember this, I will have you back one way or another. You are mine. You don't deserve anyone else. This little fling will be over and you'll crawl back to me crying your eyes out. I'll take you back, because I am not cruel to animals, to the ugly little dogs on the street. I'll take you back and you will regret rebelling against me. I can't wait."

"Get out." Alora's angry voice exploded in a way Dillon had never heard.

"Make me, whore." Wendell's ugly, low voice made Dillon's fists clench again.

"I will call the police on you Wendell, if you don't get off this property right now."

"You dirty little bitch. You can't threaten me." A hand reached out and grabbed Alora by the arm yanking her towards the porch. Dillon moved through a haze, before he'd even thought the action through.

He stepped into the doorway and growled. "If I were you I'd remove my hand from her. Before I do it for you."

"And who the hell are you?" Wendell glared.

Dillon suppressed his surprise that Wendell looked so normal. He stood just over six foot tall and had light blonde hair, with classic features twisted in anger at the moment. He wore a dark suit jacket with a purple tie comfortably, and he was big, taller than Dillon with a broad chest and thick arms. The sight of his extra-large frame beside Alora's small stature started Dillon's anger all over.

"I'm Dillon, the owner of this house. Now let Alora go, and get the hell off my property."

For a second Dillon didn't think Wendell would listen as his pale green eyes flickered between Alora and him. Then suddenly he let her go and backed away.

"This isn't over Alora. You can hide behind all the men you want, it's me you'll come back to." He warned as he turned on his heel and strode off the porch.

After Wendell reached the sidewalk Dillon turned to Alora with concern in his eyes. "Are you all right?"

Her eyes were bright with anger as she snapped. "You had no right to interfere. That was my fight." She hissed. "I can take care of myself."

"I know that Alora." Dillon held up his hands. "I was just trying to help."

She turned and stormed into the house muttering furiously as she went. "I didn't need your help. I had the situation under control."

"Under control my ass." Dillon followed her. "The moment he laid his hands on you, the situation was most definitely not 'under control' and yes I stepped in. I don't understand why you're angry at me."

"You had no right to step in. I could have handled him. If I needed your help I would have called you." She snapped.

"And when would that have been?" Dillon fumed. "When he hit you? When he finally raised his fists at you, instead of just his words? Or would you have just sat there and taken it? Like you obviously did for your whole relationship?"

"You know nothing about my relationship with him."

"No, I only know you left me for that piece of shit and that he verbally abused you. And quite frankly that's more than enough."

"I can take care of myself dammit!" Alora yelled.

"I know." Dillon stayed calm in the face of her anger, even though she obviously wanted him to yell back.

She spun around and planted her fists on her hips. "Just how long were you eavesdropping?"

Dillon dropped his eyes, not wanting to admit how much he'd inadvertently overheard. "Not long."

"Dammit Dillon." Alora wailed tears filling her eyes that she ignored. "I am a grown woman. I don't need you to protect me. I am perfectly capable of taking care of myself."

"I know that." Dillon started. But the furious look she sent him stopped him in his tracks. Confusion filled him at the anger she had turned on him, he didn't know how to react. He had been trying to ensure her safety. To make sure Wendell didn't hurt her. He didn't think he'd overstepped his bounds, but obviously he'd done something to upset her.

"So I guess you heard everything." Alora spat. "How horrible I am in bed? How weak and stupid I am?"

"Listen, that guy was a total douche puppet." Dillon moved towards her but stopped at the look of hurt on her face. "I don't believe anything he said. You may be reserved in bed, but you certainly aren't a cold fish."

Alora refused to make eye contact. Instead she mumbled. "That's just code for 'you suck in bed' I know. You agree with Wendell."

Dillon moved closer ignoring the murderous look coming from Alora, instead getting right into her face, his emotions taking over. "Don't you dare put words in my mouth. Or assume to think I am anything like that shithead. I would never call you stupid, or think that you were incapable of living on your own and surviving without a man to take care of you. I would never call you cold or bad in bed. I may wish you took the initiative more often, rather than waiting for me to start. But that doesn't mean I think you're bad, cold, or frigid. Dammit Alora." His voice rose even though he tried desperately to remain calm. "You rock my world. You are beautiful. Smart. And great in bed, reserved but great nonetheless. You drive me crazy with lust – AND it's not going away anytime soon." He took a breath and continued calmer. "Before you assume you think to know what I am thinking or 'really saying' talk to me first. I am nothing like your verbally abusive jerkoff of an EX husband."

Alora blinked once, and then stared at him for a long time in silence before she turned and walked out the back door to her studio.

Chapter 9

She was so furious that Wendell had shown up and embarrassed her so badly. How he could think that she would possibly go back to him astounded her. Add to that the fact that Dillon had walked in and heard all her dirty laundry aired. Her face still burned with shame.

Then he had so gallantly tried to help her and get Wendell to go away. Although the actions spoke of a sweetness, it also bordered on overbearing and somewhat insulting. Her anger at Dillon masked the fact the soul deep horror that overwhelmed her.

Pressing a hand to her belly in an attempt to stave off the nauseousness that had filled her when Dillon thought he had to step in to save her. Add to that he now knew just how disturbingly low her ex-husbands opinion of her was. She knew she didn't have much experience or confidence in bed and now Dillon knew it as well. The fact that he admitted he wanted her to have more initiative just confirmed everything she felt about herself. Hearing Wendell call her names didn't shock her anymore, but knowing that Dillon had heard those disgusting comment made her want to weep. And it hurt her more than she thought possible. Everything had been going so well and having Wendell come to ruin it doused her hopes and dreams as quickly as anything she'd known.

She slammed into her studio and paced over to look at the partly completed sculpture. Her eyes criticized the piece and she almost picked up the clay, then she thought better of it. Working on her art right now didn't bode well for the piece. She needed to calm down.

She stalked over and threw herself onto the dilapidated couch that stood at one end of the studio. Her sketch book in hand, using charcoal she angrily sketched for a long time barely paying attention to what she drew, just allowing her mind free reign. Her hand finally cramped and she tossed the pad of paper aside.

Taking a deep breath Alora stood again and moved to the big piece in the middle of the room. She took a moment to gauge her mental status and deemed herself nowhere near as angry or destructive as she had been when she first came in. She glanced again at the eight foot wide by eight foot high piece.

Still in the process stage, the metal armature showed a basic structure of what would eventually come to life beneath her hands. A life sized scene of a young couple holding hands in front of the symbol of the bank. Surrounding them stood smaller structures meant to symbolize all that the bank could do for them.

At this point rough didn't begin to describe the piece. The details would come as she continued adding the clay. She had started with the larger pieces. The sculpture of the woman had already been blocked out with only detailing left to do. Once she finished the entire piece would be cast in bronze which would bring all of the little details to life.

The man was a basic wire stick figure. It looked like one of those artist dolls. Tilting her head to the left, Alora could see the art coming to life. She could see what it would be when she finalized it.

Calmer, she began to knead the clay on the large metal table that stood to the side. She took large pieces and began to block out the man's legs, letting her mind drift and her creativity take over.

It felt like hours later that she shook out her hands, allowing feeling to return to them. She stepped back and admired the line of the man's calf. She turned about to grab more clay when she noticed Dillon leaning against the counter. How the man could possibly look as good as he did astounded her. His dark blue denim jeans molded to his thighs perfectly making Alora's libido stand up and sing. His blue button down shirt had the sleeves rolled up revealing forearms that were well formed and powerful. When she finally dragged her eyes up to his face she had to remember to breath. His eyes looked sad and his normally smiling beautiful mouth serious.

"I didn't want to disturb you." He said quietly.

Alora moved into the kitchenette and rinsed her hands without responding. She sighed heavily then turned around as she dried her hands on the nearby towel.

"I'll be the first to admit I don't know much about art, but it's looking good." He motioned at the piece.

"It's still in process." Alora shook her head modestly. "I've got a long way to go."

A silence stretched across the room as they looked at each other.

Dillon broke first. "I'm sorry I yelled earlier. You certainly didn't deserve that." Dillon continued in the same tone of voice. "The thought of what you must have gone through in the past nearly kills me. And while I want to be a modern man, I can't help it, I want to protect you. I felt like beating on my chest and yelling when I saw him dare to put his hands on you. I want you to be the modern woman, who can definitely handle herself, but I also have these Neanderthal urges to scoop you up and save you from anyone who might have an inkling of malice towards you. I will try to contain my inner caveman but I cannot guarantee it will happen. I also want you to know you don't have to face all your demons on your own. I've got your back if you'll let me. If you need me, I am here."

Alora allowed a small smile to flit across her lips. "I'm also sorry. I overreacted. I shouldn't have taken my anger at Wendell out on you. I was….embarrassed that you heard all of the crap he said." She hung her head.

"Alora, look at me." Dillon's insistent silky voice waited until she looked up and met his eyes, taken aback by the pure heat she saw there. "I am not Wendell. I would never believe anything he said. Ever. You are nothing like the woman he thinks you are."

"Thank you." Alora whispered.

"I do think we need to talk some more, however."

Alora's heartbeat sped up with trepidation. "About what?"

Dillon moved smoothly over to the old couch and sat. "About us, our past, and why things happened the way they did."

Alora's breath caught in her throat but she maintained an outward appearance of calm as she pulled up a chair and slowly sank onto its hard surface. She had known this conversation would come up at some point and had dreaded it. But the moment had arrived and she had to face it. Terror filled her at what he would think of her if he discovered all her secrets. If Dillon hated her afterwards that would be the payment that life extracted for her past choices. She just had to be an adult and face the music.

"You look as though you're facing the Spanish Inquisition." Dillon joked obviously trying to lighten the mood.

Alora didn't smile she just said softly. "No matter what we talk about can you promise me that you won't kick me out? I need to finish this sculpture and as you know I am against the wall."

Dillon shook his head. "Kitty, I promise that nothing you say could make me that much of an ass. You have a home here for as long as you want. I don't think this conversation will change anything. I just think it's the proverbial elephant in the room. Once we get this over with, we can move on."

Alora nodded, unconvinced but willing to give it a shot. "What do you want to know?"

"Everything. What happened? Why did you break up with me?" His voice questioned.

Alora took a deep breath and started talking. "I was young. And stupid. That's the crux of the entire situation. It started right after you moved away. Do you remember Sarah?" Dillon nodded; Sarah had been Alora's closest friend through public school. She had never cared for Dillon, feeling that he lowered the duos chances at popularity. "Well Sarah was on my case constantly. Even before we broke up, but more so after you moved away. She harassed me about you, how you didn't fit in, and how she and I could be popular if only you weren't in the picture. You were a geek, you were at college and probably dating someone else anyway. Constant bugging. Peer pressure at its finest. Then one night while we were out at the fall fair we met Wendell. He seemed so nice, so suave and debonair; everything a young girl hopes for. Sarah thought he hung the moon, and that it would only raise our image if I would date him instead of you. He started calling me the next day."

Alora sighed. "A seventeen year old is very easy to manipulate, they believe all the lies, the misdirections. I missed you so much, but you were fading. At seventeen a week feels like a month and a month feels like a year, I don't want to make excuses but it felt like it had been so long since I'd seen you. Wendell was a charming, older man. A college graduate interested in me! Average, plain jane me. He showered me with attention and in a moment of weakness I relented. I sent you that horrible letter, and started dating Wendell."

"I've regretted sending it ever since. Even if we were to breakup, you didn't deserve that mean and cruel letter. I knew it was the wrong thing to do, I should have told you face to face or at least on the phone, I just couldn't. The thought of facing you tore me apart. I wouldn't have been able to go through with it. I was also seventeen. I don't hold that as a total excuse for my behavior, but it is what it is."

"I won't go into details about dating him it's enough to say the shine from Wendell had started to fade by April of my senior year. I had applied to all sorts of colleges, intending to go into the arts and I knew I needed to get out into the world, to experience life and maybe become a mature woman who didn't cave under pressure and who could stand for what she wanted, not listening only to what others think is best for her. When I had finally built up the courage to break up with him I found out I was pregnant."

She paused and looked at Dillon's face. He looked back at her, shock evident in his expressive green eyes.

Alora continued. "I've always been one to step up to my responsibilities so I told Wendell about the impending baby. To my surprise he seemed okay with it. We discussed all our options and decided that getting married was the right thing to do. I graduated, still hiding the pregnancy from everyone, and we got married the next day. I moved into his home, his life and found out what kind of man I had married. He was a mean bugger from the start. I knew that I had made my bed and had to lay in it and I always hoped if I did things right, became the woman he truly wanted that he would change. I tried so hard in the beginning. It never worked, but the impending baby gave me hope, gave me the will to continue to fight. I couldn't wait to be a Mom. The first time I felt the baby move inside me, it lifted my spirits. Nothing could be so wrong with the world if I got a tiny human to take care of. Even if my marriage was shit at least I'd come out of it with a child to love." Alora hung her head in silence for a moment while she built up the courage to continue.

"I was seven months pregnant when Wendell came home from a work function late one night. He was drunk as a skunk, and I tried to help him up the stairs to his bed. He got belligerent and pushed me, he didn't mean to, but it happened. I fell down the stairs." Her emotionless voice hid the deep pain that stabbed her as she told the story. "I still remember the blood, it splattered on the walls and the pain was so intense I thought I would die. I crawled to the phone and called an ambulance. Wendell had passed out when they took me to the hospital. The baby died. I fell and my precious daughter was gone. The doctors stopped the bleeding but they couldn't save her. Due to complications that I barely understood at the time, and still don't really get now, I had to continue with the pregnancy. The doctors couldn't remove the child without risking problems. So for the final two months I carried my deceased child within my womb. I went into labor November sixth, right on schedule, ten hours later I gave birth to Talia."

A tear escaped and fell down her cheek as her voice cracked, the emotions finally showing themselves. She forced herself to continue. "I got to hold her, my perfect beautiful baby for a while until the doctors took her away. I named her Talia Cathleen. But she was dead. Wendell couldn't be bothered to be there. He had gone to Vegas with some friends, claiming he couldn't stand the thought. And that there was no point in his presence since the child had already died."

"Alora." Dillon's choked voice interrupted but she shook her head and continued.

"Please let me finish. I buried Talia and tried to make the best of things. I fell into a deep depression for a long time but Wendell didn't believe in therapists, so I suffered alone. I pulled away from my family and friends and isolated myself. I became the wife Wendell wanted, but he still couldn't find happiness with me. After a few years, I tried desperately to get pregnant again. It never took. According to my doctors there's nothing wrong with me physically I just have never gotten pregnant again. My baby had died within me and the Gods, fate, whatever, decided I didn't deserve to have another chance at being a Mother. Another failing of mine I guess. Eventually I became worn down believing myself to be the stupid, insipid, fat cow that Wendell told me I was. I never worked because he didn't want me to. He dismissed my art as juvenile and a waste of time, so I stopped doing it. I was a miserable twenty something home maker with no children to stay home for. Then two years ago, Wendell left me. He had found a nineteen year old bimbette named Heather to make him feel like a real man."

"It took me months of therapy and self-exploration to discover the happiness I felt when I wasn't with him. Wendell leaving me turned out to be the best thing that could happen. I reconnected with my family and my art. I found that I liked geeky things, that within me stood a proud geek. I found myself."

Silence stretched between them for long minutes while they both absorbed her revelations.

"Kitty." Dillon stood and swiftly crossed over to her, dropping to his knees so that he could wrap his arms around her. "I am sorry that you had to go through all that." He brushed at her hair in a calming manner while she let the tears flow as she rested her forehead on his chest. "I don't feel any different now than I did before our conversation. I had let go of the anger and feelings of betrayal before now. You breaking up with me, while harsh, spurred me to change. To become the man I am today. I'm not happy that we broke up or that you went through such a shitty time but it made us both who we are now. We both have grown from the past."

Alora half nodded still leaning against Dillon, almost slipping off the chair until he swooped his strong arms under her legs and around her back and picked her up. He moved over to the sofa and sat with Alora still cushioned in the comfort of his embrace.

Her tears flowed; the release that followed baring her soul had cleansed any remaining grief that had been pent up inside her. She cried for her lost baby, for her lost youth and hopes and dreams, and she cried for the lost relationship they had had. She didn't sob uncontrollably just allowed the tears and the pent up emotions of the last ten years loose. A torrent flowed from her silently.

Eventually even grief has to fade, and exhausted the tears slowed just as she slipped into slumber.

Dillon allowed Alora to sleep. Gently touching her hair and soothing her as she made soft distressed noises. He found himself overwhelmed by the revelations of the past hour, but also in awe of the pure strength that Alora had shown. That she had come out of such trails so strong amazed him.

He hurt for her, what she had gone through since they had dated felt like a light saber ripping his heart out. The fact that Wendell had treated her so foully angered Dillon to say the least, he had had everything Dillon had ever wanted and he had treated her like garbage.

He knew she would never completely get over the loss of her baby but Dillon hoped she had found some peace. While shocked to learn of it, he never put the blame on her, as she obviously did. He had never experienced anything like this so he was feeling a bit out of his depth and prayed he could support her the way she needed.

Incredible relief had flooded Dillon to see that Alora's spirit wasn't broken by her experiences. That she still could be such a wonderful, warm woman encouraged him. She would come through her experiences all the stronger.

After her confession, Dillon wanted her all the more, wanted her with a passion that scared him. He wanted to be with her as her boyfriend. He wanted the right to defend her and protect her and show the world that they were a couple.

It had taken all his self-control to not blurt out that he loved her. It had come to him in a spurt when that asshole had laid his hands on her, Dillon loved everything about her. He knew she wasn't ready to hear it. He had to let her come to him, let her decide they were meant to be together.

Dillon would be patient and wait until Alora was ready. He looked at her face as she shifted. The beauty that Alora possessed only became more prominent as she slept. The perfection of her softly parted pink lips, even the smudges under her eyes, while they gave evidence to her tears, were a sign of her inner strength. Her mind had to be the most stunning part of her; the fact that she could create such beauty out of her imagination astounded him. He glanced over at her sculpture quickly, before returning his attention to her. This woman in his arms had to be his; he couldn't stand it if they were parted again.

His arm had started to fall asleep but he refused to move. She needed the comfort and she felt so good next to him that he would put up with a little pain.

It had been nearly a half hour since she drifted off when she shifted and slowly opened her eyes. The sapphire depths nearly undid him as they came into focus on his face.

He smiled and leaned over to give her a light kiss before murmuring. "Sleepy Kitty. Are you feeling better?"

She nodded and fought her way up to a sitting position beside him. "Thank you for listening."

Dillon ran his finger down her jawline. "Anytime."

They sat together in silence for a long time, just holding hands and thinking about their reactions to the conversations of the day. Eventually the spark that existed between them started to arch back and forth. Dillon ran his thumb slowly over the back of her hand, reveling in her soft skin and the way she made him feel just being next to him.

After a few minutes, she licked her lips, the pink tip darting out to touch the plump bottom lip as her eyes stared at him. He felt his loins tighten at the sight and held his breath.

"So," She whispered, "you want me to take the initiative more?"

Unable to tear his eyes away from her lips Dillon just nodded.

"I haven't done it, take the initiative that is, very often. I want..." She fell silent.

"What is it you want Kitty?" Dillon murmured.

"You." She smiled softly. "I also want to try; I just don't know how to start."

"We could start by going inside, going to the bedroom." Dillon nearly vibrated with the lust that always burned below the surface when Alora inhabited the same space as him. The fact that she had started their encounter turned him on more than he dared admit. Her endearing self-doubt made him want to smile and he vowed to make it as easy for her as possible.

"No." Alora shook her head. "Right here. I want to be able to look over when I am sculpting and know I had you here, gloriously naked."

"All you had to do was ask." Dillon laughed low in his chest. "So what would you like me to do?"

"Stand up." Alora commanded.

He stood so quickly he almost fell over in his haste. Alora giggled, then focused and looked up at him from her seat on the couch, seriously. "Now, here's the deal," she said, "hands behind your back. No touching unless I tell you otherwise. And don't move."

Her hands slowly traced their way up his chest, weaving a pattern down his arms and across his stomach, leaving a tingling in their wake.

"I know you normally like to be in control." She whispered as her finger tips found their way beneath the surface of his shirt and touched his abdomen lightly. "Are you going to be able to handle me being in charge? Not being able to touch? Or taste?" Her low, sultry voice teased.

"I'm sure as hell gonna try." Dillon growled clutching his hands behind his back.

She removed her hands and tilted her head as she looked up at him. "Hmm." She sighed. "You don't seem to think it's going to be much of a chore. Maybe I should make it more of a challenge." She slowly raised the hem of her t-shirt and slipped the red cotton over her head. Her breasts were barely encased by the tiny white bra covered in red cherries.

Dillon groaned and closed his eyes briefly; the sight of Alora sitting there all pretty in her teeny tiny bra nearly unhinged him. She looked up at him from under her lashes and smiled. Her hands continued to slowly run over her stomach, edging closer and closer to her perfect mounds.

Dillon couldn't have looked away if a nest of trolls had appeared beside him, so entranced did those tiny hands make him. She slowly leaned back on the couch, her back arched so that her breasts tilted towards him as she played with the front clasp.

He held his breath in anticipation, his heart beating faster.

"Why don't you take off your shirt?" She asked sweetly, as she unsnapped then re-snapped the clasp teasingly.

Not wanting to take his eyes off her, Dillon grabbed at his shirt and tore it off breathlessly. Then he quickly put his hands behind his back once more.

"Good boy." She smiled, then let the snap go and slid the bra down her arms to puddle on the couch behind her. Her fingers skimmed over the top of her hardened peaks, lightly running around her nipples and stopping occasionally to tug lightly on their surface.

A groan escaped and Dillon realized it had come from him. She once again smiled triumphantly and sat up. Her hands reached around to cup his behind, her breasts pressed against his thighs. The tip of her tongue traced along his stomach muscles, leaving a wet trail. She nipped lightly at his hip bone; all the while her fingers kneaded his ass.

Slowly, until he thought he would yell with impatience, her hands moved back around to trace along the waist line of his jeans finally reaching the zipper.

Her left hand traced over his very evident erection while her right one popped open the button and slowly tugged the zipper down. "Looks like someone is enjoying the moment." She murmured as she pushed his pants and boxers down around his ankles, effectively hobbling him.

His erection jumped towards her, almost as though greeting her but she ignored it. She slipped her finger inside her mouth and withdrew it reaching up to trace around the flat disk of his nipple until it puckered as tight as her own. Then her hands slowly slipped around his back holding him steady as she licked a path down his stomach.

Dillon held his breath as Alora rested her cheek against his stomach her eyes meeting his. "Okay?" She asked uncertainly.

"Hell yes." Dillon asserted. "Any better and I'd die."

She lowered her eyelashes and smiled before she suckled a particularly sensitive spot beside his belly button. She sighed, her breath teasing his overly sensitive skin.

Slowly, with excruciating care she lowered her mouth to his erection, licking a path straight up the sensitive underside causing Dillon to jump, groaning her name.

He nearly lost his balance when she finally took him into her moist, hot mouth. She stroked deeply never breaking eye contact, while taking as much of him inside her as possible then slowly released him, flicking her tongue over the tip.

"You taste so good." She sighed.

She then repeated the process. Agonizingly slow, she moved on him again and again. Each time she took more of his erection into her mouth until she held his entire shaft inside her hot mouth. Then she swallowed and her throat muscles caused him to yell uncontrollably. His hands flexed into fists behind his back, barely able to resist touching her.

Her hands rested lightly on his ass and she began to move faster and faster, taking less of him but the increased speed, the warm wetness of her mouth had him unable to resist thrusting his hips slightly.

"Alora." He whimpered. "If you keep that up, I'm going to come." His balls were tight against him and he felt the lightheaded sensations that told him just how close he was.

She removed her irresistibly talented lips from him and whispered, her breath causing tingling all over his body. "I'm in control here. I say when I stop, not you."

Her one hand firmly grasped the base of his shaft and she renewed her tortuous onslaught on his penis. Her other hand reached between his legs and cupped his aching balls. With his penis buried deep in her warm mouth she moaned, the vibrations from it caused him to release an unintelligible groan.

She half smiled around his penis and resumed her deep throating action, moaning and swallowing alternately, fast and furious she worked his erection like a lollipop. Until finally he could resist no longer, he threw his head back and felt his insides twisting with the pleasure as his body released a torrent and he came in spurts which she swallowed greedily.

It felt like hours later, he managed to open his eyes when she released his swiftly softening penis from her mouth and smiled at him angelically.

"Holy shit, Kitty." He moaned, "That was amazing."

"Thank you." She said primly sitting back on the couch and grabbing her t-shirt. She pulled it on over her head, not bothering with her bra.

"Wait." Dillon said, sitting down. "It's your turn."

She just shook her head and pulled her hair out from the neck of the t-shirt.

"You didn't get anything from that." Dillon turned towards her, his hands reaching out for her.

"I got everything I wanted: including inspiration. That was for you." She stood up then leaned down and pecked him on the lips, her small but perfect breasts swaying under the shirt enticingly. "You know that was something else. You are something else."

She stood and moved towards her sculpting area as Dillon pulled up his pants.

"Are you sure?" He asked doubtfully. "I'll gladly return the favor, or if you give me a minute to recuperate we can continue."

She again shook her head. "You've inspired me, I've got to sculpt. I'll be in later."

With that she looked at him with a big assed grin on her face and turned towards her artwork. Dillon smiled back, loving how comfortable she appeared, and that she could do her own thing without worrying about him. She constantly amazed him, and he found himself growing more attached to her with each passing day.

He watched her for a few minutes as she grabbed pieces of clay with intent before he let himself quietly out of the studio and made his way back into the house, already planning his payback for when she came to bed.

Chapter 10

"Alora, over here!"

Alora looked in the direction of the voice and gave a one-handed wave at Cass as she made her way through the crowded restaurant.

The Sunrise Grill, a local breakfast joint that seemed to be filled to capacity. Its open concept made it overly loud and it always bustled with activity. The aroma of bacon surrounded Alora as she passed the long bar style counter filled with patrons who came alone. A few older ladies cast looks at her blue tipped hair before apparently judging her as relatively normal and returning to their meals.

Alora sidestepped a tray laden waitress with a small smile as she managed to plunk herself down on the bench seat across from Cass.

"Hey." She grinned. "Busy place today."

"Crazy." Cass smiled back. "I ordered you a coffee."

"Awesome. I'm dying." Alora sat back, momentarily regretting her late night first spent sculpting before retiring with an overly affectionate Dillon. She swore they had nearly set the sheets on fire the action of the evening had been so hot. Her legs were still somewhat Jell-O like now.

Shaking her head to disperse the erotic images, she grabbed the sugar and added four of them to her steaming cup of caffeinated heaven, figuring if the coffee didn't jumpstart her, the sugar rush would. With a sigh of joy she sipped slowly turning her eyes to look at her sister.

"So, what's the what?" She asked.

Cass looked tired, her normally wide eyes drawn, with dark slashes under them. She hunched over the table as though trying to disappear.

"Nothing." She mumbled and played absentmindedly with the cutlery in front of her.

"Bullshit." Alora leaned towards her. "Talk to me."

"Really it's nothing. I've just been dating this guy and he's turning into a total shit. I'd tell him where to shove his crap if he wasn't so damned good in bed." Cass grinned.

"Really." Alora frowned. "If he's treating you like crap, drop him. No one is good enough in the sack to be worth being an asshole outside of it."

Cass shook her head. "No, he's not an asshole, just…it's nothing. We had a disagreement the other day and I'm just venting. It's all good."

"Okay, so what's his name? I gotta check this dude out. Make sure he's good enough for you." Alora asked.

"Uh uh. Not gonna happen." When Alora frowned, Cass continued. "I need some time to figure out what's going on before I set the pack of wolves, also known as my family, on him."

Alora closed her mouth on her retort as the waitress in her mid-forties came over. Her long black hair had been pulled back in a braid that hung half way down her back, and the name tag on her chest proclaimed her as Natalie.

"Good morning ladies. Ya'll ready to order?" She pulled a much abused pad of paper out of the apron at her waist along with a blue bic pen.

"Sure." The Sunset Grill had always been one of their go to places, only surpassed by the Tim Hortons, so Alora knew what to order without looking at a menu. She looked in question at Cass who nodded her agreement.

"Shoot." Natalie poised her pen over the pad of paper prepared to make the necessary short form notes.

"I'll have two eggs, over medium, with sausage and home fries. Oh and rye toast." Alora stated, just as her stomach growled reminding her how badly she needed the sustenance.

Natalie nodded, her worn blue eyes crinkling at the corners as she turned to Cass. "And for you?"

"Same, except I'll take bacon and white toast." Cass gathered the ignored menus and handed them to the overworked waitress as she rushed off.

"Alright. So if you didn't want to talk about your love life. Why did I have a demand performance for breakfast this morning?" Alora turned her attention back to Cass.

"Well," Cass hedged. "I've hardly seen you."

"I'm not ignoring you, I've been busy. I only have five weeks left until the sculpture is due. And I have to get it to the bronzers before that."

"I know that." Cass said sharply. "But that doesn't mean you don't eat. I just wanted to catch up. See how you're doing." Her voice turned sly. "Living with Dillon. How's that going?"

Alora dropped her eyes, hoping Cass wouldn't notice the telltale pinkening of her cheeks. "Oh, you know. I've been working a lot. I haven't been able to pay that much attention."

"Bullshit. I remember how you were with him in high school. You were never happier than when you were dating Dillon." Cass sipped delicately at her still warm coffee. "So are you interested?"

"I'm not looking for a relationship. I'm still trying to get on my feet." Alora stated quietly.

"A good relationship will help you get on your feet, not toss you to the floor." Cass said with authority. "It's definitely been long enough since Wendell; you should be getting back on the proverbial horse."

"Whatever." Alora tossed her head back. "Since when did you become the love guru?"

"I'm not. I can give advice with the best of them though." Defensively Cass sat back and crossed her arms over her chest. "I've read all the articles on relationships in Cosmo. Trust me that makes me an expert."

"Hardly. But I'm not one to talk." Alora laughed.

"So has he made any moves on you? Even though you aren't looking to buy a car doesn't mean you can't kick the tires a little."

Alora desperately fought the blush that started to stain her cheeks again as she thought about how well she'd had her engine revved last night.

"Oh my God!" Cass exclaimed loudly, drawing looks from the neighboring tables. She shrugged and lowered her voice slightly. "You are doing him! Aren't you? I knew it!"

Alora refused to answer so Cass continued excitedly. "I can read you like a book Alora; you are doing the nasty with big, tall, strong geek man. So is he any good? Is he better than you remember? He's gotta be better than boring old douche cookie Wendell. Are you guys, like, dating or what? Because I have to say that would be great."

Alora held up a hand to cut her off then whispered at her fiercely. "For God's sake Cass, keep your voice down." She took a deep breath. "I'll tell you but you have to promise to keep it to yourself." Cass nodded her agreement emphatically.

"No running to any of the siblings." Another nod. "Okay then. We are sleeping together." Alora admitted.

"Whoop! Whoop!" Cass reached across the table and high fived her, ignoring the dirty looks coming from the other diners.

"Sh!" She muttered with a half laugh waiting until Cass had quieted down before continuing. "We may be doing the deed, but we aren't dating. It's been so long since Wendell left me; I needed some…satisfaction,"

"The kind of satisfaction you can't achieve with two AA batteries, you mean?" Cass interrupted, to which Alora nodded grimly, then continued.

"We have some crazy chemistry. He's seriously hot, as in steaming cuppa man hot, so I, well, I propositioned him."

"How so?" Cass cocked an eyebrow.

"Told him I wanted to be friends with benefits until the sculpture is done. He agreed."

"Alora! That is so unlike you!" Cass whispered, leaning into the conversation. "You go girl!"

"But now, I'm wondering if I made a mistake." Alora sighed.

"Mistake, why? He's not satisfying? Or is he one of those awful premature men? Does he have tiny wood? An odd affection for fetish? Bad manscaping? What is the problem?"

"No, thank god no." Alora's laugh bubbled out. "He's, well, I'm not gonna get too graphic, but let's just say wow. Wow. Wow."

"Thank you for the lack of visuals: that would fall into the realm of too much information. So if he rates three wows, what's the mistake?"

"The mistake is me. I'm getting attached." Alora leaned her arm onto the table resting her chin in her hand. "Dillon is great, we get along so well, both inside the bedroom and out, better than I could ever have hoped for. I think I might want more than casual, more than something that is over in four weeks and three days. I think I want to try a real relationship with him."

"So tell him that."

"I can't. He signed on for a sex buddy, and seems really happy with the temporary arrangement. He's doing me such a favor, both letting me stay at his place and helping with my confidence," she cleared her throat, "in the bedroom. It's not his fault I think I'm falling for him again."

"Falling for him? As in, 'in love' with him?" Cass used false quotes in the air.

"Yeah." Alora frowned. "I think so. I don't know. It's just so crazy. When I'm with him I'm happy. He inspires me and supports me. When I'm not with him I'm thinking about him and can't wait to see him again. He's," she paused in thought, "he's great." She finished somewhat lamely, unable to adequately express her feelings.

"That certainly sounds like love to me."

Alora nodded sadly. "After all the shit I went through with Wendell, I never thought I'd fall in love again. I think I've gone and pigeon holed myself, telling him I wanted a simple uncomplicated hook up and now I'm trying to change the rules. It's not fair to him."

Cass reached across the table and touched her sister's hand before speaking. "I'm glad you are moving on. You deserve better than Wendell. You always did, but you aren't the type for a one night stand, or a quick scratch-the-itch arrangement. If you think you are in love with Dillon, for God's sake, tell him. How do you know he's not feeling the same thing? You'll never know if you don't at least talk about it with him."

"I know." Alora agreed softly. "That being said, I don't think I can at this point."

"Okay then, you still have almost five weeks left, why not let it ride? See how things go and you can talk to him later about it."

"That's true. I like your idea. Procrastination always wins. Maybe in that time I'll get some sign, a signal from him that he's interested in more than casual."

"And if not, you've got almost five more weeks of awesome, earth shattering banging to enjoy." Cass grinned.

Alora laughed. "Can't beat that." The sisters fell silent for a minute both drinking from their cups as they thought about the conversation.

"I have a confession to make though." Cass broke the silence.

"Uh oh, this doesn't sound good."

"Do you remember Dillon's friend Randy?" Alora nodded, unsure of the direction of the conversation. "I ran into him, back in July. We got to talking." Cass paused.

"Tell me you didn't sleep with him! He's a married man." Alora exclaimed.

"Ugh, God no." Cass made a face. "Not my type. Anyways. He told me that Dillon usually went to Fan Expo. You had already asked me to make your costume, and I didn't know what to make. So when Randy mentioned that Dillon had dressed up as Batman for the last few years, I thought I would make you Catwoman. And if you happened to run into each other, great, if not, no big deal."

"Okay. So you made me Catwoman in the hopes that I would find Dillon and rekindle our high school romance?" Alora wasn't sure whether to be offended or appreciative. After all Cass's diabolical plan had worked.

"Not exactly. I hoped you'd run into him, and maybe talk. And if you didn't, no big deal, you still got a kick ass costume out of the deal. One that looked unbelievable on you, I might add. But you've told me again and again to butt out of your love life, and here I went again sticking my nose where it didn't belong. I'm sorry. I promise in the future to use my devious skills for good and not evil. I also swear I'll involve you in any conniving that I do from now on. Please tell me you're not mad at me?" Her eyes implored Alora to forgive her.

"You did do an amazing job on the costume." Alora conceded, debating internally whether to make her suffer with her guilt for longer then decided against it. "It's okay. I'm not angry after all, your evil scheme worked. And I got laid, which has certainly helped with my disposition."

They laughed as Natalie arrived with their meals.

***

The doorbell rang just as Dillon closed his computer. He looked absently at his watch wondering who would be ringing at five on a Wednesday. Since Alora hadn't come in from the studio yet, he made his way to the front hall. He opened the door and looked down into the smiling light brown eyes of Mrs. McIntosh.

"Dillon." She smiled widely and juggling the package she carried into one hand she gave him a one armed hug. "It is so good to see you again." She murmured.

"Mrs. Mcintosh." Dillon started, a little shocked by the warm welcome from Alora's mom. In high school he'd always had the impression that she didn't particularly care for him.

"Oh stop calling me that. You're not a teenager anymore, call me Fatina." She backed away and smiled again.

"Fatina then." Dillon returned her smile and motioned her inside. "I'm afraid Alora is still in her studio. I can go get her if you'd like."

"No. That's alright. I don't want to interrupt her if she's creating. I know she doesn't eat right when she gets into her art so I brought some treats." She held up her Tupperware package.

"Would you like a cup of coffee and we can wait to see if she finishes up?" Dillon asked politely.

"That would be great. Thank you Dillon."

He led her towards the kitchen explaining some of the work he had been doing on the house, with Aloras help. Fatina seemed impressed, exclaiming over the beautiful wood work.

Once in the kitchen she took a stool while Dillon used his newly purchased Keurig to make coffees for them both.

He turned back to the island and handed the older woman her coffee. Even in her fifties Fatina still held the same level of attraction as a woman much younger. At five foot four, her slightly rounded curves only emphasized her soft beauty. She had the same type of body as Alora. Her style however couldn't be more different. While Alora preferred form fitting jeans that showed off her beautiful pear shaped ass. Fatina always wore long flowing dresses and skirts, very hippyish. Even as a teenager dating Alora he couldn't remember seeing Fatina in anything except the comfortable tie dyed skirts and soft blouses.

Dillon pulled his mind from the past and focused on the present, looking at Fatina over the lip of his cup.

She cleared her throat. "I was very sorry to hear about your Mom. I know it has been a while, but you have my condolences. She was a wonderful woman, a devoted mother."

"Thank you." Dillon smiled, while it still hurt to be reminded of his mom, it also helped to know that others remembered her.

"I believe she did enough in this life to move up the karmic ladder in her next life." Dillon nodded. "I hope that brings you some peace."

"Again, I thank you." Dillon smiled. "Are you still working at the bank?"

"Oh of course, they'll drag my dead body out of there." They both laughed and made some small talk, before a somewhat awkward silence filled the space. Fatina looked at him with intensity as though measuring him.

Dillon couldn't take it any longer so he spoke. "I'm sorry that Alora isn't here. Are you sure you don't want me to get her?"

"No." Fatina smiled softly. "Actually, her not being here gives me a chance to talk to you."

Dillon swallowed nervously, the noise seeming to echo through the room. "What is it you wanted to talk to me about?"

"Well, a few things. I feel like we should get to know one another better being as you're living with my daughter."

"As roommates." Dillon clarified, avoiding eye contact while he told the white lie.

Fatina frowned. "Uh huh. Roommates. Right." Her tone told Dillon she didn't believe it for one minute. "Anyways. I also wanted to talk to you about Alora."

"If you're going to threaten me about her, don't bother. Your other children already took care of that."

"Well, that's good then. Once less thing for me to do." Fatina laughed softly. "I knew I raised those kids right. But that wasn't the only reason I wanted to talk to you about her. I don't know if you know too much about the meanings of names and how much I follow that train of thought."

"I remember you always talking about numberology and all that new age stuff." Dillon replied.

"It's numerology." Fatina gently corrected him before continuing. "But I referred to the meaning of names. Before the birth of each of my children I spent hours researching proposed names. Alora means 'my dream' for that is what she truly is. My first baby girl, a dream come true. She is also a sensitive soul, who spends most of her time in a world of her own. A dream world, one might say." Fatina's eyes were soft with memory for a few moments before they sharpened and looked at Dillon.

"Now Wendell. Before she married that skunk sniffer, I warned her, as much as a mother can warn their child without alienating them. Wendell means 'wanderer'. I knew from the beginning he wouldn't be good for her. That he wouldn't make her happy. She didn't listen. The failing of all mothers is having to watch their child suffer unnecessarily."

Dillon nodded with empathy. While he didn't have much in the way of family he could easily imagine how awful it must be to have to sit back and watch someone you cared about make what you thought was a mistake.

"I'm almost afraid to ask what my name means." Dillon took a drink of his cooling coffee and Fatina mimicked him until she spoke again, seeming to ignore his question.

"Back when you two were dating, you both were too into each other, far too young to be that serious. I never disliked you as a person, even though you may have thought that I did. I just wanted her to live more before finding a guy that she wanted to spend as much time as she did with you. I have come to realize that I made a mistake. With you, she radiated happiness and confidence. Once she started up with Wendell she lost herself." Fatina drained the rest of her coffee and set the cup gently on the counter. "Since they broke up, she's rediscovering that carefree, creative individual that destiny meant for her to be all along. I don't want to see her lost again." She stood up. "So far," she used air quotes, " 'living' with you, has been very good for her."

"Mrs. Mcintosh – Fatina." Dillon corrected himself. "The last thing I want is to hurt Alora. I am trying very hard to help her out and be a friend, a person, a man she can lean on. Lean on for support without losing herself."

Fatina nodded and began heading towards the door. "That's what I wanted to hear. I believe you Dillon." They walked together through the front hall. "I know there are no promises in life. But you are helping her rediscover her will to live. The fun self she has been repressing for the last ten years. And for that I thank you. I also thank you for the conversation and the coffee. You are welcome to join us at the next family gathering."

Once at the door, Fatina gave Dillon another hug and whispered. "Your name means strong, faithful. Treat her good." She smiled and swept out the door.

Dillon puttered around the house for a while after Fatina left, going over the conversation in his head. It seemed to him that he had her unspoken approval to date Alora for which his relief was palpable. Not that her families approval mattered all that much to him, but he knew it did to Alora. Once upon a time their blessing would have meant the world to him. It would have made him feel like he fit in, like he could belong even if he happened to be the son of a poor working single mother. As a teenager he had always been overly sensitive about his lack of a father. The senior Mr. Edwards had died in a car accident when Dillon had been five years old. He had blurry images in his mind of what his father had looked like, nothing concrete. No distinct memories, just a vague hole in his life. His mother had done her best to make sure Dillon never felt left out or alone, unfortunately she had to work a lot to pay the bills.

Many times as a child he remembered watching other boys playing with their fathers and the longing he had experienced had overwhelmed him. Then the guilt would always take over, after all he knew his Mother loved him and took great care of him. She had showered him with kisses and affection all the time, nurturing him so that he was comfortable in his own skin. The nerd that had emerged when he was still young had been loved as unconditionally as if he had been a sports star.

Dillon smiled gently. His mother had loved him. There had never been a doubt in his mind. It had been almost nine years since her untimely death, finally now when he thought of her the overwhelming grief didn't always take over. Now he could remember the happier moments and not always with such a pain filled loss. The loss was still there, but not as sharp. The grief was dulling.

Being around Alora, as she spoke of her family in passing, did make him jealous. He had no one left. His Mom had been an only child and his grandparents were gone before Dillon had been born. Envy filled him at the easy comradery that Alora had with her family and even though he tried to ignore the emotion, it still existed.

He wandered into the office wondering at the morose tone his thoughts had taken. Finally he came to the realization that he missed having a family. He had friends, his life successful and filled with happiness, but he didn't have that sense of belonging that a family gave a person. His mother had always filled his life and with her gone he felt adrift. Seeing Fatina had emphasized his loss in a way he hadn't expected. He didn't wish that Alora didn't have her mother, he was envious. Not in a mean way, but rather in a sad lonely way. He wanted to be surrounded and cared for the way only family can.

With a sad smile he shrugged his shoulders and turned towards his work. He couldn't change the past, and dwelling on the unchangeable would only make him sadder. Life had dealt Dillon this hand and he would live with it. Accept it until the time came that he could change it. He hoped that with Alora at his side he would discover a life that for the past nine years had only been a distant dream.

Chapter 11

Alora backed up and looked at the sculpture critically, her artist eye looking for any inconsistency, any flaw. Slowly she walked around the piece taking in the graceful lines, the realistic scale, the flow of the sculpt. Overall satisfaction filled her when studying what she had created. It was within a day of being finished – on schedule even. She had twenty-fours left to work with it, before needing to make the mold that the bronzer would use to create the finished piece.

A noise from behind her alerted her that she was no longer alone. She turned slowly and smiled as Dillon stepped into the workshop with a rueful grin.

"I didn't want to bug you…"

"It's all good. I'm through for the night. What's up?"

Dillon stepped closer, placing his hands gently on her shoulders. "Nothing. I was just missing you and wanted to see how things were going out here."

Alora turned in his arms, regarding her work again. "Almost done. I think it needs a little more detail work that I will do tomorrow then it's ready to make my mold. The bronzer comes in three days to take the piece to his shop."

"Excuse my naivety, but what kind of mold? And what will the bronzer do? Sorry I just don't really understand the process." Dillon asked running his fingers lightly over her arms.

"I will use a combination of plaster and rubber to coat the sculpture as it stands. Then I remove all the clay and the negative is created. The bronzer takes the negative to his shop where he pours molten bronze into the negative – basically recreating my original sculpt except in metal. After the metal is cooled he removes the mold and ships the bronze piece back to me so I can buff it and remove any final issues before it is delivered to the bank."

"Sounds like a lot of work."

Alora shrugged comfortably. "All necessary steps. It's a process."

"Well I think it looks great." Dillon enthused as he looked at the clay in front of them.

"You have to say that." Alora laughed. "You're hoping to get lucky tonight."

"I may want you, but I wouldn't lie to you. I really think it is beautiful. You have created pure magic with your hands." Dillon said enthusiastically.

Alora dropped her head and whispered. "Thank you." Before he noticed her blush she started to wrap the sculpture in plastic to keep the clay moist and pliable for her final day of sculpting.

"I've wanted to ask you," Dillon spoke as Alora worked. "What's in the boxes?"

Alora looked up as Dillon indicated a series of boxes that rimmed the room. "Oh. Those." Alora frowned. "They are some of my sculptures."

"What kind? Can I see?"

"They are what I sculpt when I am not doing anything for shows or pieces like this one." She hedged.

"Okay." Dillon drawled. "You are mighty closed mouthed about this Kitty. Are you hiding something?"

Alora huffed out a breath and finally finished with the plastic wrap she turned to Dillon. "They are Dragons. I tried selling them at craft shows, it didn't go well. People only wanted my kitchen wares. I didn't sell any, I only had one person even remotely interested and she never got back to me. I guess they aren't very good."

"May I look?" Dillon cocked an eyebrow as though daring her to say no.

"Fine." Alora huffed, then turned her back and fussed a bit more with the plastic wrap desperately trying to block out the sound of a box being opened.

"Wow." Dillon's deep voice broke the silence and Alora grudgingly turned around. He held a dragon that Alora had always loved. Bright purple interspersed with silver scales the dragon was approximately twelve inches tall and eighteen inches from snout to the tip of its graceful tail.

"What's this for?" Dillon looked askance at the leather contraption the dragon had been attached to.

"It's a shoulder harness." Alora moved over and showed Dillon as she explained. "Each dragon is made to sit on the owners' shoulder, like a pet. I guess I took the inspiration from Anne McCaffery's Pern series about the smaller dragons that rode on their owners' shoulders." She paused as she reached up and attached the dragon to Dillon's shoulder, wrapping the strap over his muscular chest and buckling it to hold the sculpted lizard like creature securely in place. She murmured. "I always loved that series and wanted a dragon of my own so I came up with these little guys."

Dillon looked at his shoulder dragon with awe. "This is fantastic! I love the concept and the detail is awesome." His free hand reached out to touch the delicate lizard like face as though petting it.

"Thank you." Alora responded then smiled ruefully. "I'm glad you like him, but I think you might be the only one."

"Bullshit." Dillon stated flatly looking intensely into Alora's eyes. "You said you took them to craft shows. Obviously that was the wrong market. I'm not surprised that the type of crowd attending a craft show here in Kennedy weren't interested in dragons as fine as these. But surely you, having attended a comic convention, know the right market. You know that there is a consumer base for this product that is extensive."

Alora shrugged. "I guess so. I didn't really think about it that way."

"You should." Dillon grinned. "Our geek friends would die to have a dragon of their very own. And the nerd market is heating up, allowing more and more people to let their freak flags fly."

"I had thought about starting an Etsy page. Originally my plan had been to put my mugs and platters on it, but maybe it would be a better platform for my dragons. From what I understand that might be the best way to show the world what I have."

"Great idea! I am sure your dishes are beautiful, but people can buy plates anywhere. They aren't nearly as unique as these dragons would be. If you can't go where the geeks are let them find you. The internet is a fabulous place to allow you to showcase your work. Do you have many made?" He eyed the boxes curiously.

"I have at least a dozen. Some of the boxes are filled with other stuff. Each dragon has its own name, and I made up 'adoption' papers along with short stories. So a person isn't so much buying a dragon as they are adopting a pet."

"Brilliant." Dillon grinned. "What a great marketing tool. Is there anything I can do to help you?"

"Actually, there is," Alora paused. "Could you help me set up the Esty page and perhaps a website to link to?"

"Of course!" Dillon enthused. "I would love to. Let me see what I can come up with in the next day or two and we can go from there."

Alora's face lit up with a smile and she pulled Dillon's face closer to plant a soft kiss on his lips. "Thank you."

"Anytime, Kitty." Dillon pulled her into his arms and kissed her more thoroughly.

***

"Are you sure about this?" Dillon shifted uncomfortably in the driver seat.

"Yes." Alora took her hand off the door handle and turned towards him. "It's starting to reek of hiding something. You remember my parents always had extra people for dinner, it's expected that I would bring my landlord and friend. The longer we go without you showing up the more my family is suspecting something other than friendship is happening."

Dillon took a deep breath. He knew she was right, but he couldn't help but feel like he might want to write his final will and testament before entering the Mcintosh home. Her siblings had made it clear that they could and would torture him without compunction if he hurt Alora. And her mother had shown him in no uncertain terms that she knew they were sleeping together. He had hoped by the time they came to dinner with the family that they would be officially dating and not just bed buddies. But no, Alora had given no indication that she wanted more than the uncomplicated, very pleasurable and convenient friends with benefits arrangement they had.

He also knew that the McIntosh's had for years taken in strays. He himself had been to many a Sunday dinner both before and after they had started dating. Being in love with Alora now and unable to let anyone suspect their relationship would make this dinner all the more difficult.

Taking a deep breath, he turned to Alora. "Okay then. Let's get this over with."

She laughed, then jumped out of the car calling back to him. "It won't be that bad. Stop worrying."

"Uh huh." Dillon muttered then forced a smile on his face as he followed her to the house.

Alora swung the door open without knocking and a blast of sound rolled over them. Compared to the quiet dinners with his mom and the peace of being mostly alone in the last few years the pure volume of the Mcintoshs nearly caused Dillon to run away.

"Hey." Alora yelled as she sauntered into the kitchen. "We're here!" Dillon trailed along trying desperately not to notice the swing of Alora's beautiful ass.

Instead he forced his gaze on the full room of McIntoshs, focusing on each of their faces and smiling a greeting.

Voices yelled out a cacophony of greetings to both Alora and Dillon. They moved into the room and for a few moments even more chaos followed as hugs, handshakes and general pleasantries were exchanged.

After the crush of bodies backed up Dillon found himself seated on a bar stool with a potato peeler in hand. Everyone laughed and joked as they finished the prep work on dinner. Dillon didn't say a lot, he didn't want to draw attention to himself and instead found that he relaxed into the conversation. Just listening and answering any specific questions while surreptitiously watching Alora from the corner of his eye.

She threw her head back and laughed at something her father said as she prepped a huge garden salad. Dillon's breath caught in his throat, she looked as though she had been lit from within, she sparkled with life and joy and excitement. Everything he had ever wanted stood there wrapped in white blond hair.

"Better stop staring or someone will figure out that it's more than just friendship between you two." Dillon's head whipped around to stare at Cass as she whispered in his ear.

"What?" He stuttered. "I don't know what you are talking about."

"Oh please." She drawled. "You haven't taken your eyes off her. So very obvious that you are taken with her. And that she has seen what your sheets look like."

Dillon glanced around guiltily hoping no one else could hear this conversation. With relief he realized no one was paying them any attention.

"Cass," He started but she interrupted before he even knew what he intended to say.

"It's okay. Your secret is safe with me. I'm just glad that Alora looks so happy. Whatever is between the two of you is doing her a world of good. She is confident and excited about life again. Most will assume it's because of her sculpture, but I know better. It's you. And anything that gets her going again, gets Alora to see how special she really is gets an a-okay from me. More than that it gets a 'hell yeah'."

Dillon felt a smile start to cross his lips as he glanced back at Alora. "I am neither confirming nor denying what you say."

"I wouldn't expect you to." Cass laughed lightly. "And while I may be easy going about you doing the horizontal mambo, the nasty, bumping uglies, doing the deed, whatever you want to call what you are doing with my sister don't expect that same attitude from the rest of the siblings. If they figure it out you're in for a world of hurt. So you may want to take the smoldering glances down to the minimum."

Dillon cursed under his breath and when he looked up Cass had moved off. With a super human effort he didn't know he possessed for the rest of the dinner he managed to keep a neutral, friendly, but not over the top expression on his face.

The laughter that took place during dinner warmed Dillon. He found himself genuinely happy to be included. All the Mcintoshs made an effort to talk with him and make sure he hadn't felt excluded from conversations; they even took a turn at calling him names. When he tried for a comeback, after being called an 'infected hemorrhoid on a well-used arsehole' by Brant, everyone including Fatina booed. Apparently, 'ball sucking man whore' didn't measure up in this house.

The family had been rightfully thrilled that Alora had sent the sculpture to the bronzers and now awaited the cooling period to finish. They particularly enjoyed the website that Alora pulled up to show them what would eventually showcase her adoptable dragons. Giles turned and thanked Dillon so genuinely for helping his daughter that Dillon couldn't help the lump in his throat.

Overall the night went much better than Dillon could have hoped and when they finally made their exit, while he felt some relief, he also felt a slight let down.

"See," Alora grinned. "That wasn't so bad, was it?"

"I guess." Dillon shrugged. "Were they always that loud?"

Alora laughed without answering, and as the car pulled them towards home she slipped a soft hand onto his thigh.

"Thank you." She whispered. "I seem to be saying that a lot to you, but it means a lot that you would come and put up with my overbearing family."

"Anytime." Dillon forced himself to focus on the road and not the gentle caresses her fingertips were making on his thigh. "I should be thanking you."

Alora cocked an eyebrow in question.

"Yeah. You reminded me what it is like to have a family. You brought creativity and excitement back to my life. Before you moved in I was in a rut. Day in day out, work and hanging with friends. But not really living. You've brought me laughter and lust in a way I forgot existed. So thank you."

As he pulled the car into the familiar laneway he glanced over surprised to see a sheen of wetness in Alora's eyes that reflected the light.

"Hey, I didn't mean to make you sad." He put the car in park and twisted his body towards her, placing a palm on her cheek.

"You didn't." Alora met his gaze. "I'm glad that I can help you as much as you've helped me." She leaned towards him and placed her soft lips against his. What started out gentle quickly heated up, her hands gripping his hair at the base of his neck. Her tongue darted out and traced the seam of his lips.

With a groan he allowed her entrance and pulled her closer, passion filled him in a way that he knew he'd never experience again as Alora pushed against him trying to get even closer, her breath coming in pants in his mouth.

Raggedly, he pulled away resting his forehead against hers. "We need to go inside. If you don't stop we'll end up doing it right here."

She looked up at him with a wicked gleam in her eyes.

"No." He muttered even though his entire being begged him to take her up on the unspoken offer. "What would Mrs. Miller across the street think? I am only protecting your honour."

She frowned. "Fine. But you better hurry. First one inside gets dibs on position." Impatiently she jumped out of the car and ran towards the house. Dillon cursed and flung himself out of the car catching up to her quickly.

She squealed a laugh as Dillon swung her around by the waist setting her behind him as he punched the unlock code into the door lock.

It seemed to take forever but finally the dead lock opened and just as Dillon managed to open the door, Alora jumped onto his back pushing him inside the house.

"Ha we tied." She laughed and jumped down slamming the door behind them. Without waiting for him, she quickly pulled her blouse out of her jeans and tugged it over her head. Cocking her eyebrow at him impatiently as she toed off her shoes and shucked her jeans to the floor as her bra flew across the foyer.

It only took Dillon a moment to match her nakedness and then the two of them met in a flurry of hands and tongues and lips. Her soft body pressed against his rough one, fingers tangling in hair, breathy sighs and groans of pleasure spread throughout the space. Dillon lowered his mouth and took her rose coloured nipple in his mouth tugging the pointed tip lightly until Alora threw her head back with passion.

"Dear God, Dillon." Her throaty voice belied her arousal which stoked Dillon's own higher. Her hands reached between their bodies and enclosed his erection firmly pulling a groan from his lips. Without hesitation he backed her into the door, her fingers an onslaught on his heated flesh. "I want you. Now." She demanded and slid her hands to his shoulders, nails raking the skin lightly as they went.

Dillon spanned her tiny waist with both of his hands and lifted her up, her legs circling his waist. Their eyes met and held, as he slowly lowered her and slid inside her waiting wetness. Never breaking eye contact Dillon drove into her body. Needing to be as deep as he could possibly be, to feel her muscles contract around his penis. Again, deeper, he groaned and thrust. Alora matched him. Pushing down against him her body contracting, flushed and beautiful a sweat glistened on her face as they stared into each other's eyes and frantically chased the orgasms that were spiraling closer and closer.

Dillon grabbed the cheeks of her ass and pinned her to the door, thrusting faster and faster. Unable to control himself, like some unknown force over took him as he planted his body inside the delicious warmth of Alora. He pistoned inside her, his body filled with an unbearable pleasure as the erotic sound of flesh striking flesh echoed through the room.

Finally with a groan Dillon felt every ounce of his soul tighten inside his balls and with a primal yell he continue to thrust forcefully spilling endless streams of cum inside Alora's warmth. She also screamed and the muscles of her body tightened almost painfully around him as she too found her release.

Panting with exertion Dillon waited until he could feel his legs again before pulling away, gently lowering Alora to the ground and making sure she seemed steady on her feet before he smiled ruefully. "I guess we both won huh?"

She giggled. "I am not complaining." Without embarrassment she walked through the front hall gathering their clothes and strode naked into the kitchen where he heard water being run. Dillon followed along unable to tear his eyes from the sight of Alora naked body leaning against the counter as she drank a big glass of water.

"You are amazing." He moved closer and put his arms around her body after she set the glass down.

"Right back at ya." They stood together for a while longer as their bodies cooled and Dillon's heartbeat finally returned to normal.

Finally they pulled apart and Dillon noticed the light blinking on his answering machine. He reached over and pressed play.

A woman's tinny voice spoke. "Yes. Hello. I understand this is the number to reach Alora McIntosh at. This is Calia; we met last year at a craft show. I have an opportunity I'd like to present her with. If Alora could return my call as soon as possible, that would be great. Even if it's late in the evening I would love to hear from her." The voice rattled out a phone number.

Dillon looked questioningly at Alora. She shrugged and copied the number down. "I have no idea." She answered his unspoken question then grabbed the portable phone and moved into the family room to make the call.

Wanting to give her some privacy Dillon grabbed their discarded clothes and dropped them into the main floor laundry before trudging upstairs, he threw on a pair of boxers and grabbed Alora's silky bathrobe with Wonder Woman emblazed on the back. While he would be perfectly content to let Alora run around naked the entire evening, he knew she'd be more comfortable with a robe once she fully cooled down.

When he reentered the family room she still spoke into the phone but had grabbed a pad of paper and frantically scribbled some notes. She smiled distractedly at him and shrugged on the proffered robe as she listened to the voice on the phone.

Dillon backed away, and sat in the living room waiting for her to finish. He could hear the murmur of Alora's voice without hearing the actual words and while he thought he might die of curiosity he maintained his calm and pulled out the list of renovations waiting to be done.

Eventually Alora came into the room. A confused expression on her face as she sat beside him.

When she didn't speak Dillon asked. "So, who's Calia? And what opportunity did she have to offer you?"

Alora looked shocked as she met his gaze. "She's the lady that showed some interest in my sculpture from that craft show. She runs an artist retreat, one that not only gives artists privacy and space away from their everyday lives it also gives different classes and lectures, including day camps to local budding artists. Her one instructor had to back out at the last minute and she asked me to take over. She offered me a job." Alora's voice rose with excitement. "Teaching and sculpting full time for the rest of the summer, and a possible position next year if all goes well."

"Where is the camp?" Dillon kept his voice level but his heart sank with every word.

"It's near Morrisburg, which is on the St. Lawrence river close to Ottawa. From what I understand it's a couple hours' drive. But the job not only pays great it also includes room and board." Excitement filled her voice as she continued. "It's called The Whispering Winds,

"Oh." Dillon didn't know how to react.

Alora looked at him tilting her head to the side. "My sculpture is almost done. Our two month arrangement is coming to an end. I didn't know what I would do after this, or where I would go. Calia has given me something to move towards."

Dillon nodded and forced a smile. "It really is a great opportunity for you." His heart stuttered in his chest about to be ripped free from the cage of bone surrounding it. She didn't feel the same, to Alora their 'arrangement' meant nothing. Their time had come to an end. He couldn't tell her how he felt, if she needed to move on.

"You don't seem really excited." Alora's eyes searched his face.

Forcing himself to be happier Dillon grabbed her hand. "I am happy for you. It's everything you wanted. You can sculpt, and get your online presence up and going while still earning an income. It really is the best case scenario for you." Alora nodded with a smile and looked away before noticing the sadness on Dillon's face.

Chapter 12

Alora sighed as she scrubbed at the bronze surface, her hands working on autopilot to remove the burrs and inconsistencies from the sculpture. This stage of her artwork always made her morose; she just had to finish up the details. Endings always left Alora saddened. Almost as though she had to bid farewell to an old friend, a part of her soul had been infused into the sculpture and finishing it meant saying goodbye to that bit of her. In reality ninety five percent of her work had been completed and the delivery was scheduled for three days from now.

The job offer had come at the exact moment she needed it and she had such deep gratitude for the opportunity, she couldn't help but feel let down that Dillon hadn't objected. He hadn't said anything about continuing their dalliance into a more permanent situation. She had no choice but to move on. She had slowly repacked her meager belongings, and arranged to rent a van to move to Morrisburg. Everything of worth to her had been stuffed into boxes that she had placed in the unused spare room, ready to be loaded tomorrow, her brothers were even coming to give a hand.

After the initial discussion about the job not much had been said about her impending departure. They continued to burn the sheets up at night, Alora couldn't keep her hands off Dillon, knowing that soon she wouldn't have access to his amazing body, or his funny personality made her want to cry. However, as she had told Cass, she wouldn't beg. She had made the agreement and by God she would stand by her word.

Her parents and family had been saddened that she had to move away for the job, but at the same time were happy that she had found such an amazing opportunity and they realized it was only for the summer. They knew she would come home after, even if she went back next year, it wouldn't be a permanent move and as Brant said, it gave her physical distance from Wendell.

Wendell had been popping up whenever Alora left the house, using bullying tactics to try to get Alora to come back to him. Insulting her and saying demeaning things intended to shame Alora and return to the mindset she had had when they were married.

Alora knew better than to fall for his bullshit. Her counselor had helped her work through a lot of things, increasing her faith in herself as an artist and human being, and being with Dillon had cemented her confidence as a woman. She knew she would never return to Wendell. Her marriage had ended a long time ago and she couldn't be happier about it.

Alora shook her head and returned to the present. The burnishing cloth in her hand had become ratty looking and dirty. With a shrug she grabbed a clean one from the pile, tossing the used one into the basket at her side. She gracefully folded herself to the floor and began buffing the base, determined to focus and not let her mind wander.

Several hours later Alora sighed and stretched, a satisfying popping coming from her shoulders. It was done. The movers were coming tomorrow to take the sculpture to the bank and the cheque would be in the mail. She'd be able to pay Dillon the rent she owed him and have a small amount left in the bank as a cushion.

Pulling out her camera Alora moved around the sculpture snapping pictures to add to her portfolio. She took more than needed, knowing she wouldn't have another chance to document her creation. Finally after close to fifty shots, Alora sighed and setting the camera down, she covered the sculpture with a clean white sheet. She knew she was only putting off the inevitable. Her last night with Dillon. He waited inside.

Alora knew she had to be strong, cheery and positive and not let him see how badly her heart pulled her apart. How much she longed to stay with him. She had to hide the fact that she loved him so deeply that it would be an uphill battle moving on.

The opportunity at The Whispering Winds truly couldn't be any better. Before Dillon, this would have been everything she could have ever hoped for. Now it just meant she had to leave him. And Alora knew that it would probably be for the best. She would be busy, and not have time to wallow. She would have the chance to adjust to life alone, without running into Dillon. Without risking begging him to be in a real relationship with her.

Shaking her head, Alora straightened up; forcing a happy expression on her face she left the workshop, taking a moment to securely lock the building behind her before heading out.

A raised voice that the walls of the workshop had muted from the front of the house caught her attention. She quickened her step and the sight that captured her eyes had her squinting with confusion. Dillon stood on the porch, leaning against a post with a carefree look on his face.

"Sorry. I won't disturb Alora." He said as she rounded the corner. "She is finishing up her work and needs the time."

On the lovely slate path leading up to the stairs stood Wendell. He had a bouquet of red roses clutched in his hand. "I want to see her." He growled. Alora took a half step back ensuring that neither man could see her but she could watch them both clearly.

"I'll tell her that you were here." Dillon's voice masked a smirk.

"Go get my wife." Wendell demanded his voice containing a barely suppressed fury that Alora knew only too well from their years of marriage.

"I think you mean ex-wife." Dillon said flatly.

"I don't know what you think you are accomplishing here, Edwards. Alora will come back to me. She will always come back to me. She knows her place is with me. You are just delaying the inevitable."

"I don't think I'm doing anything. Alora is her own woman and will make her own choices. I am her friend and I support her in whatever decisions she makes. And I am pretty sure her decision to not go back to you is final."

Wendell grunted in frustration. "Listen dipshit. I married Alora. She is my wife. She chose me over you before, and she will again. I'm sure your 'friendship'" He slurred the word making it sound like a curse, "means a lot to her, but it won't last. She always returns to me. I am the best she's ever had, the best she could ever hope to have."

Dillon's shoulders stiffened as he responded. "You know what Wendell; I don't give a shit about your relationship with Alora. You screwed that up. You deserved to lose her."

"She is mine. Now be a good errand boy and go get my wife."

"Screw you. You don't own her, no one does. You should go find some more teeny boppers to screw since they seem to have the same mental state as you."

Alora watched as Wendell started to retort and decided to intervene before things went any further.

"It's okay, I'm here now." She stepped up so both men could see her. Dillon smiled at her, and sat down on the step unhurriedly, as though he didn't have a care in the world.

She smiled back, knowing this time he offered his strength but wouldn't step in unless she asked him to. She turned towards Wendell.

"Wendell. What are you doing here?"

He fumbled for a moment before his voice smoothed out and he brushed back his, as always, perfect hair. "I brought you flowers. I thought we would go out for dinner."

Alora looked at the roses, realizing once again how little Wendell knew about her. She hated roses. They were her least favorite flower, a fact she knew she had told him before and during their marriage. Ignoring the proffered bouquet she instead tackled the other part of his sentence. "I already have plans for dinner. And really Wendell, even if I didn't have plans I wouldn't go out with you. As I have told you multiple times, what we had is over. We aren't going to get back together. Not today, not tomorrow and not ever again." She hated being so blunt but Wendell just wouldn't take the hint and she was done with having him constantly around.

"Dammit Alora!" His harsh voice softened as he glanced towards Dillon. "It's time we moved past everything that happened. I want to start over. You were the only one for me, ever. Let's go talk in private. Without any outside influences."

"No. Wendell I won't. I don't want to start over. There is too much pain in our past for me to ever want to rekindle what we thought we had." Alora's thoughts turned momentarily to the baby that she had so desperately wanted, her memories of the night she fell down the stairs interspersed with carrying her dead child in her womb without any support from her husband. "We weren't good for each other. It's over." She stated flatly.

"You're talking about the baby you lost. That wasn't my fault. Accidents happen."

Alora's eyes widened with disbelief as Wendell continued oblivious to her expression. "Shit happens. You need to get over it. We were too young to have a child then. You know that as well as I do."

"I really don't." Alora frowned. "At least if we'd had a child I wouldn't have wasted the last ten years."

"Oh please." Wendell rolled his eyes. "The only reason you feel it was wasted is because you found out about me and Michelle. If you hadn't found out about that affair you would have been happy in your naïve little world. Back the way things are supposed to be."

"Come on Wendell, you know we weren't happy. Besides, now you are free to find a woman who 'is whole' and can give you a family to pass on your legacy to. That's what you always accused me of wasn't it? That I wasn't a real woman?" Alora noticed her voice raising and took a moment to take a breath.

"Having a kid never crossed my life plans. A screaming brat constantly wanting my attention? Hell no. I only said that to appease you. Honestly at first I thought the pregnancy was a ruse to snare me, your type always does that. But since it worked with what I wanted I agreed to marry you anyways. I was a little surprised when it turned out you actually were pregnant. I wasn't pleased, I've never liked children. Quite frankly I didn't mourn when you lost the baby. And I took precautions to make sure that never became an issue again." Wendell didn't temper his voice as he leaned towards Alora in anger.

Her skin chilled. "What do you mean by that?"

Wendell stopped and swallowed visibly. "Nothing." He muttered.

"Bullshit! What the hell is that supposed to mean? You took steps? What steps?" Alora snapped.

"Fine." Wendell glared at Alora, apparently having forgotten Dillons presence on the steps, or the fact that they were having a screaming match in the front yard. "I took care of it. I knew I didn't want kids so I made sure I'd never have any."

"You got a vasectomy without talking to me? Your wife?" Her head swam with the implications. She had tried for nearly a decade to have a baby that Wendell had known would never happen, and yet he let her believe that something had been wrong with her. A chill raced down her spine thinking about all the times she'd dealt with what she considered her failure.

"It was my choice. Isn't that what all you feminists go on about? My body, my choice?" Wendell's face twisted in a sneer.

"Yeah. Your choice." Alora's outraged eyes met his. "But, as a couple you would think it might be something we'd have discussed. Or perhaps that you wouldn't have lied to me about it at the very least. You let me believe I was a failure. That's how you kept me under your thumb for so long." She heaved an internal sigh of relief, not that she'd thought she'd ever go back to him, but this little tidbit of knowledge broke her completely free. The last ties to Wendell snapped, almost audibly, she had never been broken; she had choices in the future.

"Why are we even talking about ancient history, there isn't a bad guy in this situation Alora. No matter how much you want to paint me as some villain, I am just an average guy. The best you could hope for. And what we had may have had its flaws, but it was ours and we were in love."

"Maybe you aren't some crazy villain, but you aren't the good guy in this story either."

"There are no heroes in real life sweetheart. It's time you got your head out of the clouds and realized here on earth there are only men like me."

Alora shook her head, she knew that good guys existed, Dillon proved that point. He had saved her in more ways than one, and stood hands above Wendell when it came to class. "I don't believe that Wendell. There are good guys. But that is neither here nor there. I don't love you anymore. The reason is unimportant. I will never fall in love with you again. We are finished. Over. Done. I can't say it any clearer. Stop looking for me, stop trying to woe me. I'm done playing by your rules. I want you to leave, and if you bother me any more I will not only call the police on you but I will also let my brothers know. They have been aching to get the go ahead to deal with you. Now go away."

Decisively Alora turned her back on Wendell and calmly walked up the stairs and into the house with her head held high. The door barely made a sound as it closed behind her, forever cutting off the link to her past.

***

Dillon felt like cheering, watching Alora tell that weasel Wendell to go to hell had been exhilarating. She had been glorious in her righteous fury, beautiful beyond belief. While he had wanted to step in and make sure nothing hurt her, he had learned from the last time that Alora had to fight her own battles. And fight she had. She hadn't needed Dillon at all. She had been strong and unwavering. Tough and firm.

All in all she encompassed everything Dillon wanted in a life mate. And that is where the problem lay. She left tomorrow. Tonight they spent their last night together and while a part of Dillon wanted to beg her not to leave, he knew this opportunity would be wonderful for Alora. That, and he didn't think he could handle being rejected by her again. Once in this lifetime had been more than enough.

He slowly walked into the house, ignoring the spike in his chest as he passed the pile of cardboard boxes set beside the front door. He squared his shoulders determined to make tonight the best night possible, to enjoy his last moments with Alora and not let melancholy take over. She couldn't know the sadness that covered him. How overwhelmed he became at the thought of rambling around this big house alone, with her gone. He would not give in. He had tomorrow and the rest of his life to grieve. Tonight they needed to celebrate. An occasion to honor all that Alora had accomplished. Both in her personal life and artistically. All the promise that had shown in high school had come to fruition at this beautiful moment.

He took a moment to thanks the Gods that she had turned down the goodbye dinner her family had wanted and instead had opted to spend the night alone with Dillon. He hadn't planned anything special, as he didn't want to make it seem like he was glad that she left in twelve hours. He wanted to spend their last night together as they had spent the last sixty days, with laughter and passion. Alora also didn't seem to want to make a big deal of tonight being the last night, she had thrown a simple casserole in the oven and talked earlier about watching the season finale for Doctor Who. In a slight acknowledgement of the significance of the evening Dillon had picked up a nice bottle of wine and a white chocolate raspberry cheesecake for dessert.

"Hey." Dillon rounded the corner to the family room and approached Alora. "You okay?"

Alora turned, a soft smile on her lips. "Yes. More than okay. I'm relieved. I feel like I have been set free. I can't believe I let him manipulate me like that for so many years, but it is truly over now."

"Good." Dillon placed his hands gently on either side of her face. "You were magnificent. I am so proud of you."

A faint blush touched her cheeks. "Thank you. And thank you for both being there but restraining yourself and not stepping in. That meant a lot to me."

Dillon frowned slightly, dropping his hands slowly. "You didn't need me. You had all you needed inside you to get rid of that piece of trash."

"Maybe." She grabbed his hand. "But you being there gave me the encouragement and inner strength to believe in myself. Without you I don't think I would believe I had the strength. I have gained so much confidence since I moved in here that I have to thank you."

Dillon shook his head. "The strength existed inside you all along. You would have found it with or without me. There is absolutely nothing to thank me for."

He turned away, his hand sliding out of Alora's effortlessly. If the conversation continued on this train he would break his vow and spend the night waxing poetic about her beauty and begging her not to leave him. Instead he forced lightness into his voice. "The only thing you should thank me for is my cooking skills. I am a little concerned about that casserole. Are you sure it's going to taste all right?"

Alora slapped him lightly on the arm as she moved past him, opening the stove in a puff of smoke. "It's fine. Hamburger casserole always smells like this." She waved a hand in front of the stove in a valiant effort to dispel the smoke.

"Uh huh." Dillon moved quickly to the smoke alarm and disconnected it before it started with its ungodly noise. "At least if we can't eat that I bought dessert. That's bound to be edible."

"You bought it. That's cheating." Alora pulled the slightly blackened casserole from the oven, a look of consternation on her face. It made a decisively heavy sound as she set it on the trivet.

Dillon moved over and hugged Alora from behind, ignoring the bite in his nose of burnt hamburger. "Whatever it is, it will be great. I have an iron stomach and you know I'll eat anything. Now let's get it onto plates and settle ourselves in for the Doctor."

"Screw the Doctor. And the food." Alora turned in his arms, flicking off the oven mitts and placing her small hands on his shoulders. "Let's spend the night in bed."

Dillon's groin tightened, his breath catching in his throat. "Hell yes." He said firmly. Grabbing her hand the two of them raced through the house shedding their clothing on the way.

***

Alora fought off residual tears as she turned off the main highway. The drive had gone smoothly, although it had been fraught with tears and emotional outbursts. After six hours on the road, a terrifying moment or three as she sped through the horrifying Toronto traffic she had almost arrived at her destination.

Last night had been wonderful, she and Dillon had spent the night in bed talking and laughing. They eventually ordered pizza, eating it in bed with cheesecake and wine on the side. They had made love multiple times, discussed everything from politics to their hopes and dreams. The only taboo topic (by unspoken agreement) had been the following morning and what would happen when Alora left.

It had been a beautiful, sad way to conclude their agreement. With laughs and lovings. And when the dawns light had touched the room Alora had drifted off to sleep tucked safely in Dillon's arms. In her dreams she and Dillon had been in an official relationship, not a friend with benefits agreement, and she vaguely recalled the feeling of completeness, of absolute happiness that had surrounded her. Unfortunately the alarm went off and she abruptly got yanked from the dream and thrust into reality. She had to leave.

Her brothers had shown up bright and early to help her load the van, bringing the whole family with them. Even Daxia and Eric had driven home to help in a show of Mcintosh solidarity. They had laughed when Alora suggested she didn't have enough stuff to warrant all six of them coming and explained in no uncertain terms that she couldn't escape without a Mcintosh goodbye. It had been loud and boisterous, with an edge of sadness on the laughs. They had made quick work of loading up then spent a good fifteen minutes giving hugs and goodbyes. All the while Dillon had stood on the porch looking at her with hooded eyes.

Finally the moment arrived. Her family packed themselves into their vehicles and drove off with loud honks and waves. Alora waved until the cars had disappeared from sight before turning tentatively towards Dillon.

"I guess it's time." She spoke, her loud voice shattering the silence.

Dillon nodded and stepped towards her. His arms wrapped around her and he whispered into her hair. "Thank you. This has been the best sixty days of my life and for that I will always be grateful."

Alora nodded into his shirt and fought back tears as she whispered. "It's been…" Alora paused not wanting to lead the conversation into her making a fool of herself finished lamely, "…fun."

After an eternity that would never be long enough she pulled away. "I should get on the road."

Dillon nodded and opened his mouth then closed it firmly. Finally he smiled and spoke. "Drive safe. Lets' get together when you get back to town."

"Sure." Alora swung herself up into the vehicle and smiled at Dillon before cranking the key and driving off with a, hopefully easy going, wave.

She had made it four blocks before her tears had blinded her, forcing her to pull over. But as with so many things in her life Alora pushed through.

The gravel road crunching beneath her tires pulled Alora back into the present and she blinked her eyes. The GPS had warned her how close her destination was and she slowed the vehicle, executing a smart right turn into the parking lot.

After six hours of driving Alora's back screamed with relief when she finally got out of the van to stretch. As she worked out the kinks a woman came out of the small outbuilding that flanked the parking lot.

"Alora?" She asked. Alora nodded and the woman walked gracefully over to her. "I'm Calia." She held out a hand.

Alora smiled and shook her hand. Slim, bordering on skinny Calia had long black hair pulled up in a simple high pony tail. Her dark eyes assessed Alora frankly. "How was the drive?"

"Okay I guess. I'll admit I'm not a fan of driving through Toronto."

Calia stepped back with a grin. "I'll totally agree with you on that. If I never have to drive in the city again it'll be too soon. You look a bit frazzled, why don't I give you the quick and dirty tour and then let you get settled in."

"Sounds good."

"We don't drive gasoline powered on the property. Everyone has access to solar powered golf carts so let's hop in I'll show you around then we'll come back to get you unloaded." She waved a hand at a two-person cart that had been parked beside the out building.

"Okay." Alora grabbed her purse and keys from the seat pushing the lock button as she hopped into the golf cart that Calia had pulled up.

Calia laughed, waving a hand at the open forest that surrounded them. "Not many people out this way looking to steal a vehicle."

"Sorry, habit." Alora blushed.

"It's all good." Calia drove the vehicle with an expertise that bordered on insanity as she whipped around trees and followed a path that Alora hadn't noticed before.

"The retreat is a couple miles from here so why don't I tell you about what to expect while you are here."

"Sure." Alora agreed as she watched the beautiful scenery with a sigh.

"Okay, so The Whispering Winds is a retreat I built on land that has been handed down for generations in my family. I wanted to give other artists a peaceful place to relax and rejuvenate while being surrounded by nature. A place where they don't have to worry about the mundane and can focus on their work. The land borders the river on the south side, the Saint Lawrence River that is. The other three sides are surrounded by forests. There are numerous trails for walking and enjoying. I have seven artist cabins that are used by writers, painters, sculptors, whatever. I am not overly particular on the artistic endeavor so long as it is creative. I always reserve one cabin to award to a different artist each season to use free of charge. The other six are available for rent. I have my own big house – where I stay. Essentially the headquarters. You'll recognize it – it's the only two-story building on the property."

Calia took a breath and pointed through the pine trees. "If you look over there you'll catch a glimpse of the river." Alora looked and saw a slight glimmer of light reflecting off water before the view became swallowed once more by forest.

"A couple of years ago I gained a contract with a local college to offer summer courses in the arts. That's where you come in. I offer the students classes in all different forms of art from drawing to painting to sculpting. They come here to learn. At that point I built the instructors lodge. It's four individual rooms off a common living area, set a short distance from the artist cabins. Very rustic, as I warned you in the emails." She glanced at Alora and waited until she had nodded an acknowledgement of the rudimentary accommodations she could expect. "Attached to that building is a large common space where you can teach classes. That's where I've set up the kiln and ordered all your requested supplies."

"Meals are taken communally in the pavilion. We encourage the artists to join us as well as any instructors. You won't have to cook – all meals are provided. Students will also join us for lunches when they are here. It's not menu oriented. More family style, serve yourself and sit and enjoy the company. We don't cater to specific preferences, although if you have any allergies we take that into account." Calia had a way of speaking that seemed quick and to the point. She didn't seem to hedge her bets, telling Alora exactly how things were run. Alora appreciated the bluntness.

"Now as to some other touching points. Internet. We have limited access, deliberately. I want my guests to connect with nature and their muses rather than be distracted by Facebook. However I have come to realize that having some access can be necessary. So, each artist, or employee is allowed an hour access a day. I have a computer in the big house for you to use. As I said cars are a no go, but our carts can be used to run into town. The charge lets them go that distance."

"That's good." Alora finally spoke. "I have to return the rental van tomorrow and I wasn't looking forward to hoofing it back to camp."

"No worries. I've got friends who can give you a ride if need be. Morrisburg is a fifteen-minute drive from here and although it is small there's a restaurant, a grocery store and even a Tim Hortons if you need it." Calia smiled her dark brown eyes crinkling.

"Awesome." Alora grinned back. "I don't know if I could make it the whole season without my coffee."

"Well, my friend you just wait. We have the best coffee this side of Toronto. My friend, Dell mixes the dark roast beans with arabica beans before grinding them. Trust me, you will love it."

"I'll give it a shot." Alora said, doubt filling her voice, her affection for Tims coffee ran pretty deep and she didn't know if any home-made version would stand up.

"That's all I'm asking." Calia continued her previous topic pointing to a smaller path. "That leads to the hot springs. A small area that serves almost like a hot tub. I encourage you use any of the facilities here when you aren't working. I recognize that you are an artist too and you may as well let your muse soak up the atmosphere while here."

"Perfect. Just one question." Calia waited. "Are there merengue lessons? Or perhaps watermelon juggling?" Alora held her breath as soon as the words slipped out of her mouth unsure how Calia would take it, or if she would even get the reference.

Without missing a beat Calia shot back. "Unfortunately not. No Patrick Swayze neither. But I understand the comparison. Love that movie and I will admit it did sort of influence what I came up with. Maybe we'll have to do a 'Dirty Dancing' movie night." Alora grinned breathing a sigh of relief, she knew she'd fit in just fine.

Chapter 13

The past month had sped by for Alora, her students had been wonderful, and teaching had brought her more pleasure than she'd thought possible. Watching the creative awaken within previously logical, unartistic people made her smile. She had always believed that everyone had a voice. Every person had the ability to create and be artistic they just had to trust themselves and allow their muses freedom to express themselves.

The retreat was as gorgeous as Calia had touted it to be. The sunlight dappled through the trees creating a magical environment so conducive to artistic endeavors. Everyone from the staff, to the artists, to the students had been welcoming and wonderful. She had formed a deep friendship with Calia, more than she had ever expected. The owner of the retreat had the same sense of humour and interest in art that Alora herself had. They had spent many nights together around a campfire talking about everything. Although Calia appeared to be younger than Alora she found herself drawn to the woman. She had a sense of peace about her, almost like the retreat had become a true reflection of the owner.

The hot springs were a relaxing way to end the night to release any tension from her muscles that sculpting had caused, and after getting used to having them available, Alora knew that when she owned a home she had to have a hot tub. Although curiosity ate at Alora, as to how hot springs existed in this area. She had never heard of any natural hot springs in Ontario before, but she couldn't complain, she loved the sense of peace that the warm private waters.

In Alora's mind one place at the retreat stood out, she always returned to it, which gave her the most creative juice. A huge oak tree in the middle of a small grove seemed to be pure perfection. It towered above all the other trees, offered the exact right amount of shade and yet still kept her warm. The grass around it sparkled a healthy, bright green. A little crook at the base of the tree allowed her to comfortably cuddle with a sketch pad and her thoughts and lose hours at a time. To Alora it seemed like Mother Nature hugged her as she sat there. Sometimes she drew, sometimes she wrote and sometimes she just allowed her thoughts to drift into fantasies or dreams. Alora had never found an outdoor space that could comfort and inspire her as much as this tree.

Her Esty page had exploded, all the dragons that had been stored in boxes for years were adopted and on their way to their new homes. For the first time since her marriage had ended she had a healthy balance in her bank account and didn't worry about every penny. She now spent every spare hour she had making and naming new dragons, desperately trying to build stock for her page as well as to take to Fan Expo. She had a few months before the event but still worried about not having anything to show. Whenever she had a moment to spare she thought about Dillon and thanked him in her head for helping her set up the page and for giving her the courage to apply as a vendor at Fan Expo.

Then she changed the subject in her brain before she thought too long on Dillon. Keeping busy during the day kept her mind from drifting. But at night when alone in her room, her mind always slipped towards Dillon. She had moved past the tears and now stood firmly in resignation, touched with a healthy dose of gratefulness.

She had resolved when she moved back after the summer she would ask Dillon on a proper date. She would take the step to being with him in public. If he rejected her that would be the end, but she knew she couldn't spend the rest of her life wondering what if, why, how? She had to know she had tried. She had to know that she hadn't given up, that she had taken the risk.

"Hey." Alora looked up at the voice and smiled as Calia approached.

"Hey yourself. What's up?"

"Nothing." Calia folded herself gracefully to the grass. "I see you found my tree."

Alora ducked her head. "Yeah. She's beautiful." She paused. "Um, did you want me to leave? Or even to move over so you can sit?"

A laugh escaped Calia and she brushed the heavy fringe of black bangs out of her eyes. "No, no. I can enjoy her any time I want. I'm glad you're relaxing and have found somewhere to inspire you."

"Definitely. This tree, there's something about her. I just find myself rejuvenated after being here. I keep coming back." Alora sighed. She'd never referred to a tree as male or female however in her mind this oak tree represented pure femininity.

"I'm glad." Calia looked at Alora closely. "You seem happier than you did when you arrived. I hope that the retreat is helping you as much as you are helping me by being here. Your students love you and I am ever so grateful that you were available on such short notice. We love having you here."

"I'm grateful for the work. And I am happier. I have come to some decisions about my future that I look forward to implementing." Alora said thoughtfully.

"That's good."

"Yeah. I guess sometimes distance puts things in perspective."

Calia paused, picking at a piece of grass, allowing silence to envelope them. Finally she said slowly, "How are you feeling?"

"I'm happy, healthy and relaxed. Why?" Alora's brow furrowed with concern as she thought about the tone of the question.

"Well," Calia drawled. "Normally I don't interfere in my staff's business. But I consider you more than just staff. You're a friend. And I hope you feel the same about me."

"Of course." Alora enthused. "You are a friend and I am very glad we met."

"Okay, then. So, you don't mind if I meddle for a minute?"

Alora frowned before answering. "Meddle away. And I will try not to get offended."

"Oh, I don't think you'll be offended. At least I hope not." Calia inhaled a deep audible breath before speaking. "I sometimes have this innate sense about things. It allows me to know things about people, things they themselves might not have realized yet. It comes and goes, and I have no control over what it is that I think I sense."

"Okay." Alora drawled the word unsure at the turn the conversation had taken. Although she loved the genre of fantasy and science fiction she didn't necessarily believe in that type of thing in real life. She had never experienced anything that would allow her to think that any 'innate' senses or 'esp.' existed outside of the television.

"So, the last week or so my senses have been tingling about you." She looked at Alora through her lashes. "I can tell you don't believe in that sort of stuff, and that's fine. I still want to share what I've been feeling. You can do what you want with what I tell you. If you don't believe me that's fine, it won't affect either our friendship or your position at The Whispering Winds now or in the future."

"Good to know." Alora interjected. "I can't say what I believe, because frankly I don't know. I can promise to listen with an open mind."

Calia smiled gently. "Okay then. After our many conversations I know all about Wendell and Dillon and your history. As you know about mine." Alora nodded in agreement. "I don't know if you know this or not, or really how to even say it, so I'll just spit it out. Alora you are pregnant."

Alora blinked. "Um." Her hand went to her stomach and she tried to mentally calculate how long it had been since her last period. She hadn't had one since she'd been at The Whispering Winds and before that it had been at least a month, although that she had never been very regular and couldn't rely on a calendar to know when to expect Aunt Flo. "How do you know?" She whispered, still unsure whether to believe it or not.

"I just have this way about people, healing I guess you could say. And with you I sense an extra spark of life." Calia reached into the oversized pocket on her hoodie and pulled out a small rectangular box. "I figured you'd want extra proof, so I bought one of these." She set the test down on the grass between them.

"I…" Alora floundered, stumped about how to react or what to say.

"It's okay. I know you never thought this would happen for you. Take the test and give it a few days to settle in. You have next weekend off if you want to go home and maybe have a talk with that man of yours. Or not. Your choice."

"I…" Alora still couldn't form sentences.

"Take your time. And if you need me, or to talk, I'll be at the pavilion for the next couple hours." Calia stood and with an understanding smile strode away.

***

"Seriously, you need to figure out your shit." Joe shook his head as he handed the plastic shopping bag emblazoned with 'The Heroes Den' across the counter to Dillon. "You've been moping around like a lost dwarf for the last month. It's time you either dealt with it and move on, or find her and made it work."

"Come on. I haven't been that bad." Dillon frowned unhappily.

"Bullshit." Joe said flatly. He fumbled with the cash register before turning again to Dillon. "Normally I try to stay out of the emotional advice thing, but it's so obvious you are completely taken by the girl. And Alora is great. You were happier with her than I've seen you in a long time. Why did you let her go?"

"I couldn't force her to stay. It was her choice, and the job opportunity couldn't have fit Alora's needs any better." Dillon smiled sadly. "I wanted her to stay but I also wanted to support her. She has such talent that the world needs to see, and she should take all the chances and opportunities that present themselves to her."

Joe nodded. "I totally get that. And I think you were right to not interfere with her opportunity but did you ever give her the chance to stay? A reason to not go? Or even tell her you wanted to see her when she got back?"

Dillon frowned, thinking. "No. I didn't say anything. As you know we had an arrangement, I couldn't go and change the rules part way through."

"Again I call bullshit. You didn't want to take a risk. You didn't want to get hurt again. You were waiting for her to take a chance and tell you all you wanted to hear. At any moment you could have told her how you felt."

"How do you know how I feel?" Dillon shot back.

"Please." Joe drawled. "Get your head out of your ass. I may own the geek shop, but that doesn't mean I'm blind to human interactions. It was completely obvious. It still is. You're just scared that she'll hurt you again and you wanted her to be the one to come to you."

Dillon stared at Joe for a long moment before speaking. "You know you're right. I was too afraid to be hurt by Alora. I didn't tell her anything, I let her leave thinking I would be happy with our friends with benefits agreement coming to an end." He shook his head with dismay. "So Love Master, what do I do now?"

"You go find the girl. You tell her everything you've been hiding and show her that you want to be more than a fuck friend when she moves back home."

"I've got her email. I can send her a message."

Joe punched his arm lightly. "Don't be a complete shit. You don't tell a girl this kind of thing by email. You need to go to her. Tell her in person. Make the effort." He shook his head. "I swear it's like you've never watched a romantic comedy in your life. It's called a romantic gesture."

"I…" A flustered Dillon stumbled over how to respond. "You're right. The only thing is I don't know exactly where she is. I only know it's near Morrisburg."

"Then you find out. I saw her hot sister go into the mall an hour ago. Go ask her."

"You mean Cass?" Dillon's eyebrows shot nearly to his hairline. "Hot? She's cute sure but I wouldn't say hot."

"That's cuz your blind by your luuuuve for Alora." Joe batted his eyelashes with a laugh. "Now stop arguing with me and go get your girl."

***

Alora stood nervously outside the door. The familiar porch welcomed her in ways she didn't want to admit to. Although she had planned on coming back to ask Dillon to date her, she hadn't thought she'd have to break this kind of news at the same time. Definitely not what she had originally had in mind. She had debated endlessly about how to deal with the situation ever since those two pink lines had stared back at her. The thrill she felt every time she thought about the life growing inside her only dimmed by her nerves at having to talk to Dillon.

After endlessly debating all her options she knew the only right thing to do. She had to tell Dillon. He would be a wonderful father and even if he had no interest in being with her intimately she couldn't imagine not sharing his child with him.

The thought of not admitting it, and having the child in secret held some appeal that Alora couldn't deny. The idea of running away and loving her child to pieces by herself without ever having to admit to anyone how badly she'd screwed up also enticed her. But she knew she had to do what was right, she had to give Dillon the chance to be a father, the chance for their child to know his or her entire family. So while running away seemed like a viable option Alora wouldn't do it. She would stay and fight for her future.

With a fortifying breath she raised her hand and knocked firmly on the door. Inside she could hear some movement and within a few moments the heavy wooden door swung open. Alora looked up into the face that she had come to know so well, the green eyes widening in surprise at seeing Alora on the porch.

"Alora." His voice whispered.

"Hey Dillon." Alora whispered back, fighting back a longing to push his black hair off his forehead.

"Is everything okay?" Worry flashed through Dillon's eyes.

"Yes." Alora breathed with a smile. "I came back to town for the weekend and wanted to chat with you. Can I come in?"

"What?" Dillon shook his head. "Of course. I'm sorry, that was rude. Come on in."

They went into the family room in silence; Alora sat in her spot on the sofa and then had to remind herself internally that it didn't belong to her any longer. Dillon sat on the edge of a chair opposite her, his hands clasped together as he searched Alora's face.

"I thought maybe we could talk." Alora started.

"Yes." Dillon's breath came out in a rush as he leaned forward. "I wanted to talk to you too."

"Oh?"

"I actually just accosted your sister at the mall. Demanded your contact info but she wouldn't give it to me. We kind of got into a screaming match."

Alora's eyebrows nearly disappeared into her hair. "What?"

"Yeah. Neither of us is welcome in the Chapters anymore." Dillon hung his head shamefully and Alora snorted a laugh.

"You had my email. Why didn't you just message me? You didn't have to fight with Cass to get my info. You could have just asked me."

"I had this image in my head of me showing up at the retreat in some big surprising gesture. I didn't want to give you the chance to say no."

"I wouldn't have said no." Alora whispered.

"I didn't know that." Dillon looked at her. "Do you think Cass will forgive me?"

"Not sure about that." Alora tilted her head. "She really liked going to that Chapters." She giggled.

"So what did you come to see me about?" Dillon asked.

"Well..." Alora had had six hours of driving to try to figure out what she wanted to say and still found herself no closer now than she had been when she first left the retreat. "I guess I wanted to know how you felt about maybe going on a date with me when I get back in the fall."

"You drove six hours to ask me to go on a date in two months?" Disbelief filled Dillon's voice.

"Yeah." Alora dropped her head. "I know I hurt you in high school, and I knew I had to be the one to make the move now. I want to date you. More than that Dillon I want to be your girlfriend. I know it wasn't part of the deal that we made and I will accept it if you say no. But I couldn't live my life wondering what if?" Alora's voice came out in a rush as she spit the words out. "I couldn't live with knowing I let you get away again without making an effort. At the risk of being hurt myself. I needed to take that risk. I care so much for you Dillon. I want to see where this thing between us goes. I need to know if it's one sided. Are my feelings reciprocated? I can't tell, I don't know. I just-"

"Shut up." Dillon interrupted. "You could at least give me a chance to answer." He smiled softening his words. "I wanted to come tell you that I wanted to try dating again. That I wasn't satisfied with only having a 'friends with benefits' relationship with you. I was terrified about what you might say but I wanted to make the move. But here you are. You beat me to it. And you are here saying everything I ever wanted to hear from you and it's like magic to my ears."

Alora felt her heart beat joyfully. All the things she had ever wanted to hear from Dillon were spilling from his lips.

"I care for you as well." He continued. "No, I more than care for you dammit. I think I am in love with you. You stole your way into my heart when we were teenagers and it's never been the same. I count myself as the luckiest man alive to have been given a second chance with you."

"Dillon." Alora's choked voice whispered. "I love you too." Her eyes filled with tears as Dillon jumped up from the chair and moved over to her. He dropped to his knees in front of her and enfolded her in his strong arms.

"You don't know how long I've waited to hear those words from you." He whispered into her hair.

Alora sniffed, unable to speak as she drew on the essence that surrounded Dillon. Finally after an eternity she pulled back. "I have more to tell you. And it might change your answer."

Confusion and concern warred in Dillon's eyes as he leaned back. "There isn't anything you could say that would change my mind about you."

"How about you hear me out first." Alora smiled sadly. "As you know from being around during my fights with Wendell," Dillon scowled but let her continue. "I believed I was infertile. That the miscarriage of Talia had caused something to go wrong inside me and that I couldn't ever have a child."

"That doesn't matter." Dillon interrupted. "Even if we never have any children, if I have you, that's all I need. We can adopt if that's what you want."

Alora shook her head as Dillon's voice drifted off. "That's not it. Remember that last fight, Wendell admitted he'd gotten a vasectomy without telling me. I am not infertile. Actually the opposite. I'm pregnant."

Dillon's mouth opened and closed a few times, shock filling his eyes. "But I thought you were on birth control?" He finally got out.

Alora shook her head. "No. Since I thought I couldn't get pregnant I wasn't on anything."

"Okay." Dillon sat back on his heels, his eyes trying to adjust to the new knowledge. "Are you sure?"

"As sure as I can be with an over the counter pregnancy test." Alora's heart dropped. She stood. "I understand if you don't want to be with me. Or feel that I've mislead you. I assure you it I didn't intend for this to happen. I won't ever keep you from your child, as much or as little as you want to be in his or her life. That's your choice."

She moved towards the exit, fighting tears, when a hand shot out and gently touched her arm. "Stop."

Alora turned towards Dillon. "Just give me a minute." Alora waited in silence studying his face for any sign of what Dillon must be thinking.

Finally he led her back to the couch. "I am sorry to have been so shocked. I never expected to hear something like this. I've never been told I was going to be a father before." He swallowed audibly. "If you weren't pregnant were you intending to come back to me? Or are you only here because of the pregnancy?"

"God no! Please don't think that." Alora blurted out. "I only found out last week. I had decided to come back and see if you wanted to pursue a relationship prior to that. I love you. Whether I have your child or not. I want you."

Dillon nodded with simple acceptance. "All right then. I have always wanted to have kids. The opportunity has never presented itself. I can not wait to have a child with you. But that means we aren't casually dating. I want to be exclusive. I want the relationship. I want the whole enchilada. When you finish with your summer gig I would like it if you moved in here permanently. Us. A couple. Out in the open. No more hiding how we feel. Admitting to your family that we are together. The works."

Alora nodded. "I want that to."

"Good. Glad we agree." Dillon dropped a hand to her stomach. "I can't believe you are having our baby." His voice held an awe that brought fresh tears to Alora's eyes. "I've wanted you since we were teenagers. There is no one I want to spend my life with other than you. Please tell me you feel the same and that this is long term for you as well."

"It is. I realized what a mistake I had made letting you go all those years ago, but it was too late." Her voice was soft.

Dillon smiled, "Never too late. It's only the beginning."

Other Titles By Gloria C Bishop

Supernaturally Yours

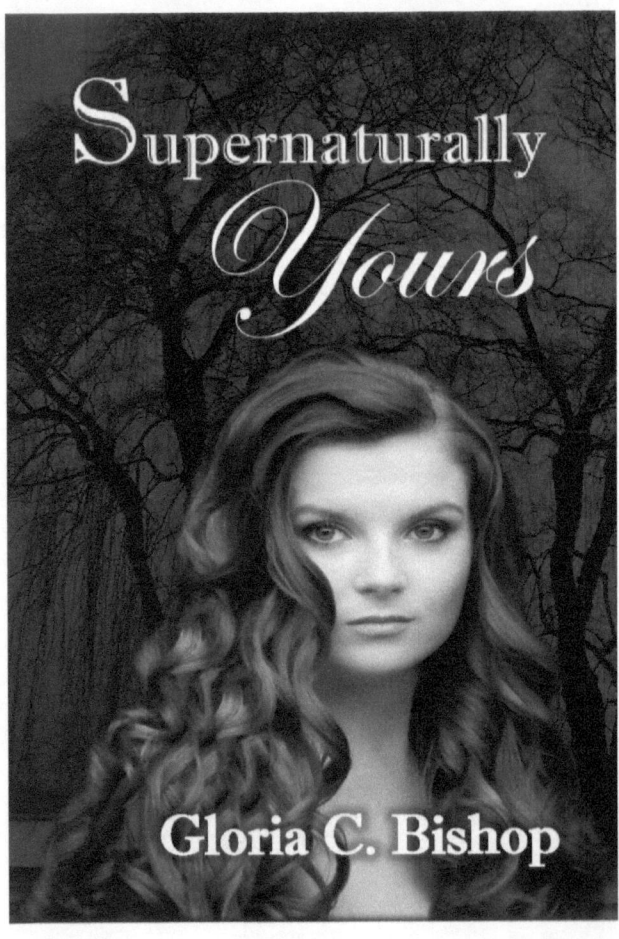

Anna is your average small town girl. She likes to cook works at a bookstore, and is quiet, and klutzy -the girl next door.

She is also a supernatural creature.

Becoming a zombie has brought her nothing but heartache. Her family life, her love life, even her self-esteem have been shattered as a result of her transformation. After sitting on the sidelines for far too long, Anna decides to begin dating again. Unfortunately her foray into the world of supernatural singledom is met with disaster.

Thrown into the arms of the one man who hurt her more than any other by a psychopath bent on her destruction, Anna is forced to reevaluate her opinion of Nathan. Their steamy chemistry is overwhelming as they discover that together the can find, and overcome, the fiend who is behind the attempts on Anna's life.

Becoming Kira

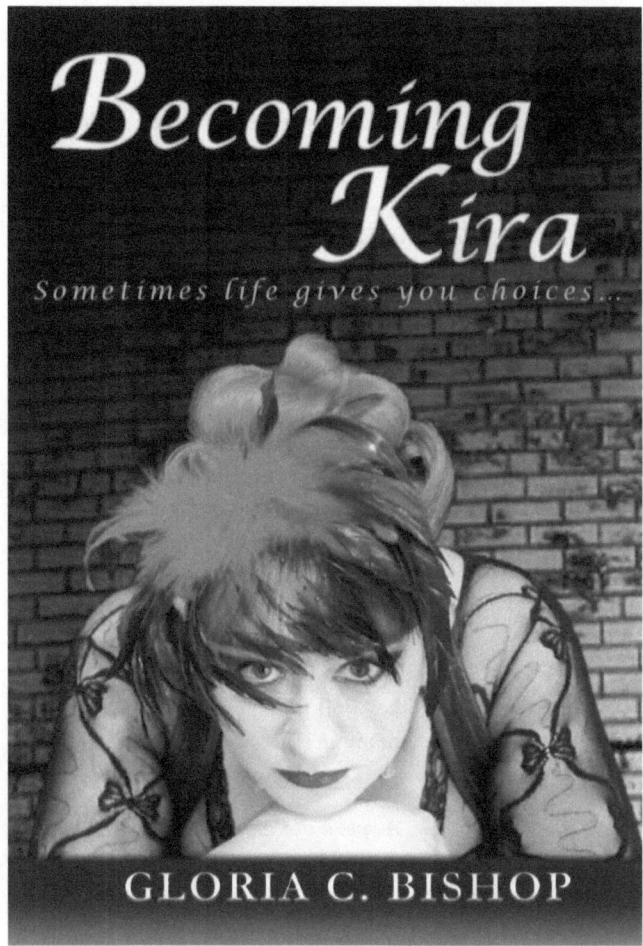

Kira always did what was expected of her. Fall in love young, get married, and settle into a normal life. That's the path, the end goal, the dream, right?

Unfortunately her whole life was turned upside down and when her husband walked out, her dreams came tumbling down along with her self-esteem. Kat never expected to be single again, let alone at thirty-eight. Now she needs to learn to love herself and rediscover the person she was meant to be.

Her first foray into the world of being single surprises her and very quickly she is faced with an impossible, but delectable decision to make, the repercussions of her selection will affect her entire future.

She changes, she chooses and finds her path, eventually

Becoming Kira

A contemporary romance novella about love and dating in a modern age.

Liquid Fire

Everyone remembers their childhood as being magical, Lee just found out hers really was.

After suffering a run of bad luck, Lee wants nothing more than to lick the wounds of her past and bury herself away from reality, but she discovers a world of magic, a history she never realized existed. Her destined elementals are being held against their will and the only way to find them is to align with the incredibly delectable, unbelievably stubborn Jeremy. They wind down pathways that will take their undeniable chemistry even higher as they move closer to the sinister plot that has stolen her birthright. Together they will find the villain and learn that sometimes fire and water can mix with steamy, hot results.

A spark of flame glows, A sprinkle of rain slows....

The Whispering Winds

Michelle wakes up knowing one thing: she had escaped hell. She wants nothing more than to keep running and ensure she'd never be caught again.

Healing minds, healings souls is what they do. It's what all Incubus and Succubus do. Dawn had to help Michelle and if it healed Mason in the process all the better. Mason had his own problems. He'd come to The Whispering Winds to recover from his own past not be drawn into more human drama and emotions.

None of them expected the heart punching connection they found together. The danger isn't over yet.

Can Dawn, Mason and Michelle come together to defeat the evil that threatens to tear them apart before they can give their love a chance?

About the Author

Gloria lives in Southwestern Ontario Canada, with her hubby, her two teenage kids and a slightly larger than normal (or believable) cockapoo named Spike. She was lucky enough to meet the dude of her dreams at a drunken toga party while at college, two days before her nineteenth birthday and they've been together ever since. She believes in romance, and that attraction doesn't have to die off. She loves to laugh with her hubby and believes in keeping a sense of humor above all else. Gloria has always written, everything from poetry to a column in a local paper. Her favorite is to write romance, because everyone deserves that feeling, that belief in a happily ever after.

She draws and collects crafts like other women collect shoes (which she also collects but that's another story) When she isn't wearing her hat as mom, wife, writer, sister, artist, daughter, crafter, doggie mommy, friend – she can be found sitting around a campfire with an eclectic group of friends.

Overall she is a scooter riding, wookie hoodie wearing fun loving woman who refuses to grow up.